MOCCASIN THUNDER

Also by
LORI MARIE CARLSON

Red Hot Salsa

The Flamboyant

The Sunday Tertulia

You're On!

Hurray for Three Kings' Day

Sol a Sol

Barrio Streets, Carnival Dreams

Return Trip Tango and Other Stories from Abroad

American Eyes

Cool Salsa

Where Angels Glide at Dawn

MOCCASIN THUNDER

American Indian Stories for Today

edited by
Lori Marie Carlson

■ HARPERCOLLINS*PUBLISHERS*

Moccasin Thunder
Compilation copyright © 2005 by Lori Marie Carlson
All rights reserved. No part of this book may be used or reproduced in any manner what-
soever without written permission except in the case of brief quotations embodied in
critical articles and reviews. Printed in the United States of America. For information
address HarperCollins Children's Books, a division of HarperCollins Publishers, 195
Broadway, New York, NY 10007.

www.harperchildrens.com

Library of Congress Cataloging-in-Publication Data
Moccasin thunder : American Indian stories for today / edited by Lori Marie
Carlson.—1st ed.
p. cm.
Summary: Presents ten short stories about contemporary Native American teens by
members of tribes of the United States and Canada, including Louise Erdrich and
Joseph Bruchac.
ISBN-10: 0-06-623957-5—ISBN-10: 0-06-623959-1 (lib. bdg.)
ISBN-13: 978-0-06-623957-6—ISBN-13: 978-0-06-623959-0 (lib. bdg.)
1. Short stories, American. 2. Short stories, Canadian. [1. Indians of North America—
Fiction. 2. Short stories.] I. Carlson, Lori M.
PZ5.M73 2005
[Fic]—dc22   2004022186

Typography by Larissa Lawrynenko
16 17 18 19 20 PC/LSCH 10 9

First Edition

Acknowledgments

My deepest gratitude to the gracious,
generous writers of this story collection.
All have shared words of friendship,
time, art, and knowledge with me.
Thank you, thank you. And also, my
appreciation to Rosemary Brosnan
and Jennifer Lyons.

CONTENTS

Editor's Note

Every now and then, on Sunday afternoons in the 1970s, when I was a junior-high-school student growing up in Jamestown, New York, my father would pack the family into his Buick and take us on leisurely rides to Salamanca.

Salamanca, half an hour's drive from my town, was known for its interesting American Indian museum. Filled with artifacts—everything from clothing to jewelry, agricultural and hunting tools, urns and vessels, baskets, arrowheads—it was dedicated to telling the story of the Seneca people, one of the six nations comprising the Iroquois Confederacy, a proud people whose legacy was— and continues to be—so strong in Chautauqua County that many of the rivers, lakes, villages, and towns bear names from the Seneca language.

The Seneca were so much a part of our local history that an entire semester of my eighth-grade social studies class was dedicated to the study of their culture. I now know that the curriculum was by no means comprehensive. I would even venture to say that it was sometimes offensive and riddled with inaccuracies. Nevertheless, we learned about the long house, the Seneca ways of cultivating crops, the importance of community and family in their lives, and their deep and abiding reverence for the earth and every living thing. Yet, for as much as we students were learning about the past, we knew hardly anything about the Seneca who were still living in our community, as well as in neighboring Allegheny County in Pennsylvania.

I remember that in my Lutheran Sunday School class of mainly Swedish-American youth, there was one girl who told us she was half American Indian. She was a quiet lady, with eyes the color of onyx, and I wished to befriend her. I wanted to ask her questions about her life and family, but I was quite shy, and she was too.

We never really got to know each other, a fact that I regret to this day. I mention this in order to encourage those who may find themselves in similar circumstances to act upon their good intentions. My inability then to overcome my reserve is most likely one of the reasons for my doing this book. This anthology is my way of belatedly reaching out in a gesture of friendship.

Later, when I was in college, I heard for the first time a song sung by Joan Baez that related an incident in my hometown region that had occurred while I was growing up: the flooding of sacred lands, burial grounds, to make the Kinzua Dam. I remember being shocked. It took Joan Baez's insightful mind and soulful song to reach me, to make me truly aware of the injurious effects of such an event upon the American Indian community in and around Kinzua. When I finally heard the anger and sadness of those upon whom such injuries had been done, I felt ashamed.

In my profession over the past twenty years, as a writer and editor working mainly to bear witness to the lives of Spanish-speaking people in the United States, I often thought of the young adults in American Indian communities throughout this country who, while being nurtured by their own families and cultural institutions, had been ignored by mainstream society.

I began to look back on my youth and realized how much I, as well as all the students in my junior high school, had missed by studying only a small part of the American Indian past—as interesting as it might be—for there is so much in the present that is exciting, deeply moving, spiritual, and very worth knowing. To that end, I thought to put together a book of American Indian voices that tell their stories *today*.

As the reader travels from one region, one heart, one finite space to another and another in the following pages, I hope that many worlds will unfold in the rhythms and paces of the present as well as the past, and will linger in the peace of understanding. The generous writers of this collection have offered us their wisdom, and it is to them, especially to the late Lee Francis, a rare treasure of a man, that this book is dedicated.

Introduction

What a wonderful time to be an American Indian! In Indian country, on reservations and in urban communities all over the United States, a great awakening is in process.

In the field of education, the great tribal colleges movement is growing increasingly powerful as a tool to change communities and people. In film, one American Indian director after another turns his or her camera on powerful Native stories. In the visual arts and sculpture, some of the best work in the world is being created, and the power of American Indian literature is singing through the world with ever-increasing crescendo forces.

Throughout Indian country, the efforts of many Indian nations to preserve and grow cultures and languages is enabling us to explore new philosophies and ways of being through the lens of tradition and history. The American Indian condition—with all of its historical pain and the glory of its powerful civilizations, now caught too often in the grip of poverty—is being examined with increasing sophistication and depth.

The American Indian stories in this collection are part

of the river of awakening reshaping not only Indian country but also American literature as a whole. Sometimes the stories achieve the impact and cadence of the powerful oral traditions that helped American Indian people build civilizations long before Europeans came to this planet.

In Joy Harjo's wonderful "How to Get to the Planet Venus," two young women face the dilemmas inherent in the contemporary Indian experience, as poor choices and alcohol lead to a powerful climax of guilt, shame, redemption, and the deep humanity of American Indian people. The story's poetry is as sharp as the "slender knife" of the moon "in the dark winter sky."

Sherman Alexie's "Because My Father Always Said He Was the Only Indian Who Saw Jimi Hendrix Play 'The Star-Spangled Banner' at Woodstock" is raw and unrelenting in its realism and language. This is not a story meant to comfort you or make you feel better about the universe. The main character says at one point, "I was conceived during one of those drunken nights, half of me formed by my father's whiskey sperm, the other half formed by my mother's vodka egg." The story confronts the reality of an absent father who is needed by his son in ways almost too deep to express.

In "The Last Snow of the Virgin Mary," Richard Van Camp tells the story of a dope dealer who has the finances of his business down cold but has no clue about how to put his life together into an acceptable future even though he has dreams and a plan. Cynthia Leitich Smith, in "A Real-Live Blond Cherokee and His Equally Annoyed

Soul Mate," confronts the complex tangle of who American Indian people are in a society bent on stereotyping. The magic in Joseph Bruchac's "Ice" is as powerful as the "great dark wings" of the eagle in the story that cups the air and "flaps up, glides, flaps again with an ease unrivaled by any human-made flying machine."

The important point is that the contemporary American Indian awakening is made, as these stories are made, of deep contemplations about a past that is still alive in those of us who are descended from ancient peoples. The contemporary world presents us with endless dilemmas. Some of these are from the larger society: drugs, alcohol, racism, the confusion of being of mixed race. Some of the stories are painfully personal, dealing with incest, the failure of a father, the love of a mother, the humanity of a school official who bends the rules in order to help the young women she is responsible for become all they can be. Some are poetic and true, reaching into the heritage of civilizations that understood humor and relationships and the natural world of which they were citizens.

This collection includes Louise Erdrich's enchantment. "Wild Geese" explores, like all of these stories, the trembling edge of adulthood. Human innocence and the glory of the relationship between man and woman are placed in the context of powerful emotions. These emotions dangle in a swirling stew of greed, righteousness, fear, shame, honor, and generosity, each emotion following another in a rapid dance of meaning. The language dances with images and a calling back to tradition and history and a movement into the timelessness in which all of us exist as human beings.

We can name the authors of these stories: Joy Harjo, Cynthia Leitich Smith, Louise Erdrich, Sherman Alexie, Greg Sarris, Joseph Bruchac, Richard Van Camp, Lee Francis, Susan Power, and Linda Hogan. They are a song inside the river of time; they speak with power of that moment when we are no longer children, but are not quite adults. Still, we carry the heritage of the ancientness of our peoples inside of us. We hear the echoes of wisdom inside the drum of the words in these stories that fill up the blankness of paper, and then fill our spirits, our hearts, our understanding.

Beauty. Reality. Harshness. Love. Forgiveness. Redemption. Remembering. Awareness. Singing. Confusion. Dancing. Failing. Growing. Hatred. Pain. Surviving. Reaching. Becoming. Being. Ways of being. Thinking. Feeling.

Ah, we are lucky to be alive at this time! In spite of the pain and confusion, the making of mistakes and over-coming of mistakes. An awakening is under way, and we have the honor of being able to hear the voices that are giving song to this new day!

—Dr. Helen Maynor (Scheirbeck)—
Lumbee
Assistant Director for Public Programs
National Museum of the American Indian

MOCCASIN THUNDER

How to Get to the Planet Venus

JOY HARJO

I used to fly to the moon. I never had to think about it; it just happened. This was before I went to school and learned that I needed a degree in aerodynamics to understand how to get from here to there.

One night the moon was full, bright with an aura of ice as earth headed toward winter. My father hadn't come home again, and my mother waited in front of the television, the blue flickering glow turning her back and forth between light and dark. It had become more difficult to leave for the moon because I never knew what would happen, what he would do to her.

The luminescent road to the moon was strong and familiar as I made my way to the old man who was my guardian there. We did not need words to talk. That night he took me to a quarry of stones, and we walked down to the edge, where the scrap pieces were piled together.

Below it we could see the world I had come from. Across town my father was coming out of Cain's Ballroom with a blonde woman on his arm. They were kissing and laughing. We could see my mother doze as the television screen blurred, and then the baby awakened and she went to him, changed his diaper, and held him close to her neck as she turned the light on in the kitchen to make his bottle.

This was the first time we had come here to this place together. I knew then that this would be the last time for a very long time I would see the old man, and I felt sad. We watched the story as it unwound through time and space, unraveling like my mother's spools of threads when I accidentally dropped them. But I would not recall any of it for years.

I returned at dawn, and my father showed up with smeared lipstick on his white shirt and the terrible anger of a trapped cat. Not too long after, my father left us for a dancer, and my mother immediately married a white man who didn't want children. I was sent away to Indian school.

The moon was a slender knife in the dark winter sky. We huddled in the ditch behind the boys' dorm, passing around a bottle of sticky sweet cherry vodka. It kept away the cold and the ghosts of sadness, and after a few sips I was free. Next to me was the new student, Lupita Bear. I had to keep from staring at her. She was beautiful. Her perfect skin was café au lait, and her black eyes were elegant like a sacred cat's. She announced she had checked out the male population of the school when she arrived earlier in the week and was giving a report.

". . . And what's the name of that Sioux guy with the geometric painting designs? With the nice smile and perfect back, always running touchdowns between classes?"

"John Her Many Horses," we chimed. We'd all noticed him.

"That one over there." She motioned to Herbie Nez. He was Navajo and slim as a girl. "He's much too pretty. I could eat him up in one bite!"

Herbie's hearing was like radar and tuned in to everything, even the songs and cries of spirits who hung around the school. In the past, children had been dragged there against their will. He looked over at us and batted his eyelashes. We all laughed as we downed the next round. Then suddenly our party was over. The dorm patrol surprised us in the nearly moonless night, and we scattered into the dark to save ourselves from detention, restriction, and being sent away.

I ran until I couldn't run anymore. By the time I made it back, my roommate had already been caught, judged, and tried, and was packing her bags for home. She was the first that semester to be kicked out of the dorm for drinking. She was to be the object lesson for all of us.

Her family came after breakfast the next morning, just as a light rain blew in over the mountains. We all watched apprehensively from the dorm living room as her father stiffly lifted her suitcases into their truck to take her back to Dulce. When she climbed in next to her mother and brothers and sisters, she turned and waved a heavy good-bye.

That night Georgette Romero woke up the whole dorm. First I heard her screams and then running as she fled down the hall toward my room, which was in the farthest wing. Lupita saw everything, she told me later, because she was up writing a letter to her mother at four A.M. When Georgette ran by, she was being chased by a ghost the color of sick green. Her roommates refused to let her back into their room and burned cedar to dispel the evil. No one wanted the girl with the ghost, but since I had the only extra bed it was decided she move to my room. That night and for many nights after, I stayed alert in the dark and didn't sleep, anticipating the return of the ghost.

Now Georgette's books were all over the floor, and her plastic beauty case spilled over with makeup and polishes, flooding the counter we were supposed to share. For hours she scraped and rubbed off chipped polish on her nails, then reapplied numerous thick coats, smelling up the room with polish and acetone. She left used dabs of cotton and underwear scattered on the floor. At first I was amused at this alien creature, told myself that she had made herself her own canvas, but she was getting on my nerves. I spent more and more time in the painting studio or sat on the fire escape listening to music.

This afternoon when I came in from school, I couldn't hear anything for the whine blasting from Georgette's favorite country station. I had just been summoned to meet in half an hour with the head dorm matron, Mrs. Wilhelm, and after the weekend I had every reason to be afraid. I needed to think quick. If I was kicked out, I could not go home. I had to make a plan about what I would do, where I would run.

"Hey, I need that!" Georgette gestured to me with her nail polish applicator as I turned down the volume, almost muting it. "I had a rough day."

"Peace," I said, turning up the music a notch, then opened the windows to let in some air and to relieve the panic. I wouldn't go back. I would kill myself first.

Across the way, from the boys' dorm, I could hear Herbie Nez practicing his guitar. He was my other eyes, my other ears, and we shared a love for jazz, Jimi Hendrix, and esoteric philosophies.

"Our dark sides are compatible," I told him one night as we flew to Jimi's guitar, far from the dancers in the center of the gym, far from the school, from pain.

"Hmmmmm . . . ," he answered. "True, as true as horses breathing clouds in winter."

"Perfect," I answered.

And then he laughed and I laughed. We fit, though he was born in a hogan and didn't speak English until he was sent to a Catholic boarding school, and I was born in a city speaking English. My father's language was a secret he used to speak with his relatives, the ones who hated my mother. She looked white, and her relatives had signed the treaty for our tribe's removal from our homelands. That treaty was still fresh, though the signing was almost

5

two hundred years ago. Herbie's spirit gleamed and spun and called to me to climb higher and higher. And with him I always could, fearlessly.

Georgette was in love with Clarence, Herbie's cousin from the other side of the Navajo reservation. Clarence was one of those shy-eyed Navajo men with big eyelashes and a tight, tapered back. He lived for rodeo, for the ride, be it with horses, bulls, or girls. Georgette's mood fluctuated according to her sightings of Clarence. She had been trying to lure him all semester, and he was the focus of her beauty tricks.

"So Clarence didn't bite today?" I asked.

Georgette glared at me. "That Mexican girl better go back where she came from, is all I can say," she snapped.

"You mean the opera singer," I answered. Lupita Bear wanted to be an opera singer, went the rumor, but the idea of any of us becoming an opera singer seemed so preposterous. It was wildly possible, just not likely. It was probable that most of us would become cosmetologists or car mechanics, move back home, and have babies.

Sitting in the ditch last weekend she didn't look like an opera singer; she was one of us. She had laughed as we ran through the dark from the dorm police. I could still hear it—a trained laugh—and for a moment I could imagine her as an opera singer, far away from here on a stage where her looks and shine could amount to something. She was gorgeous, and she didn't have to try. She was half Mexican, and her father was from a tribe in Oregon I had never heard of until I came here. The word was this school was her last chance.

Last night Herbie told me that Clarence had made a bet he could have her within a week, that she would be easy. All the boys were watching to see what would happen and were placing bets. "Did you place a bet?" I questioned Herbie.

"Of course not," he had answered. "However, I'm placing a bet that I'll have that Lewis Jim wrapped around my fingers by Saturday night."

"Yes, the most improbable candidate for your love in the whole school."

"I like a challenge," he quipped.

We laughed at the incongruity. Lewis was Clarence's best friend. He rode bulls and even looked like a bull. He was square to the earth and prided himself as a stud and would probably beat Herbie up if he caught Herbie staring at him in public.

Georgette didn't know about the betting, and I was tempted to tell her, but as much as I was growing to dislike her, I didn't hate her.

Lupita's singing pulled me up the hallway as I prepared to meet my doom in Mrs. Wilhelm's office. She was singing along with KOMA radio, on a signal that flew straight across the plains all the way from Oklahoma City.

I stopped to listen with everyone else who was within hearing distance. Her voice was a living, breathing thing, like Jimi Hendrix's guitar, like Jackson Pollock's paintings. My father told me that some voices are so true they can be used as weapons, can maneuver the weather, change time. He said that a voice that powerful can walk away from the singer if it is shamed. After my father left us, I learned that some voices can deceive you. There is a top layer and there is a bottom, and they don't match. Like my stepfather's voice. The top layer was jovial and witty and knew how to appeal to those in power. The bottom layer was a belt laced with anger and terrible desire for the teenage daughter of his wife, my mother.

Everyone clapped when the song was over.

"Forget opera," I blurted out, "you can sing anything you want." Everyone turned to look at me, including Clarence, who was leaning against the wall, pretending he was an innocent audience member.

"Hey, thanks," she said warmly. "Do I know you?"

We had met at the ditch. Maybe she had forgotten, then I saw her eyes move sideways toward the dorm assistants, who were listening to everything. We couldn't be too careful. Maybe she, too, was waiting for Mrs. Wilhelm.

"I'm Lupita, from the planet Venus." She smiled at me, aware of the rapt audience of high school boys who all snickered when she made reference to the planet Venus.

"I'm Bonita, Creek from Oklahoma. Oklahoma is a long way from Venus."

Though she was my age, she seemed suddenly older as she slid her hands self-consciously along her tight sheath skirt. Her nails were long and painted, the look Georgette strived for but would never get. In that small moment, I felt sorry for Georgette. She didn't have a chance.

"Do you really like my singing?"

She glanced over at Clarence, who gave her a shy dance of his eyes. It was obvious that Lupita had a thing for Clarence. There was a light that jumped between them, an electrical force so strong that it sparkled in the late afternoon sun. Who was after whom? I wondered.

"Lupita, can you move your admiration society outside?"

It was Mrs. Wilhelm. I had briefly forgotten about her. She motioned me into her office with her determined chin and sharp gray eyes. Suddenly I was afraid again. The door shut with a precise click. I sat at the table I had shined with lemon wax just that morning. My detail was to clean her office after breakfast before going to school. I did so diligently, with respect and fear.

"I have something I want to show you," she said. Here it is, I thought. I expected her to pull out last weekend's report detailing the ditch episode, or at the least point out an uneven wax job. Instead, she put a letter in front of me.

It was addressed to Mrs. Wilhelm, and it was from my stepfather. I had no idea why my stepfather would write Mrs. Wilhelm or the school. I had never seen him write a letter to anyone. His routine was to come in from work at four, find a reason to hit me, then read the evening paper. My mother would hide in the kitchen cooking dinner, though she was tired after waitressing all day at the diner for the old lady from back East who ran the place.

Once I lost it. My mother was exhausted from working a double shift. My stepfather sat in his huge chair barking out orders. He yelled at my mother to cut his meat, to bring him another glass of iced tea. Then he snapped at her because she wasn't moving fast enough.

"Hurry up, bring me some more ice! What's taking you so long?" He had just asked her for something at the other end of the house a few minutes before.

Before I could put the brakes on I said, "Why don't you buy her a pair of roller skates so she can get around faster?" I was belted, then grounded forever. But it was worth it, like a thunderstorm cleaning evil and leaving a satisfied land.

I took out the letter. The envelope had been opened neatly by Mrs. Wilhelm with the electric letter opener I dusted every morning. He had used my mother's drugstore stationery and had written neatly, sanely, with blue ink in a voice of careful authority.

> *Dear Mrs. Wilhelm,*
> *I am writing to you because I think there are some things you need to know about our daughter who is now a student at your school. We had quite a problem with her when she was in our home and could not control her. Watch out for her. She will lie to you and she will steal. She is not to be trusted.*

I was not his daughter, he had never called me daughter, nor had I lied to him or stolen anything. Tears threatened, but I refused to give him that satisfaction, even six hundred miles away. My face blushed, stung by betrayal. He was the liar. He was the one who had stolen; he had stolen my mother's life and was attempting to steal my reputation. I stuttered, but nothing came out.

Mrs. Wilhelm told me, "This is what I think about this letter," and she tore it up into pieces and threw it in the trash can. I was relieved. It had never occurred to me that it was possible to be trusted over the word of a white man who belonged to the Elks Club. As I left her office, I promised myself that I would not drink again. She had believed in me, had given me another chance.

That was the first shock. The next shock was walking into my room to find Lupita sitting on my bed while Georgette struggled to pull on my prized fake suede hip-hugger bell-bottoms. They were stuck at her hips. Everyone on our floor shared clothes, though they usually asked permission first. Georgette had not asked.

"Excuse me!" I shouted over the radio just as she triumphantly snapped the top button.

"They fit," said Georgette smugly as she pushed a chair up to the mirror over the drawers and climbed to admire herself front and back. "Do you mind if I borrow them?"

I stole a look at Lupita, who was absentmindedly sifting through Georgette's box of polishes. "Aren't they a little tight?" I asked.

"No, they fit perfectly," Georgette said. So, in the name of making friends with Lupita, I momentarily let it go, wincing as I watched Georgette make furtive swimming dance movements as she watched herself in the mirror.

"Be careful, and you'd better not dance in them," I reminded her as she hopped down.

I was still blown away by Lupita's voice. Her kind of talent was rare and burned bright. She had a chance. The school was paying for private music lessons, she told us as Georgette pulled out her nail polishes and picked out what I thought was a horrible color for Lupita.

Lupita humored her, but she was no fool. The music teacher, however, wasn't just teaching her to sing. She laughed as she told us about his wandering hands as he put his arms around her to demonstrate abdominal breathing.

"So where is your mother from?" I figured I might as well find out the answer directly.

"Venus," she said. "She's from Venus, so I come from the planet Venus." She was serious.

It was then I remembered the old man, and how I used to fly to the moon. I remembered the quarry of stones and my mother holding the baby. I remembered my father. I felt lonesome, like my belly was being scraped by the edge of sorrow.

She and I talked about everything, about our fathers, about the ability to fly in dreams. Georgette listened quietly as she polished Lupita's nails. She volunteered nothing. I told Lupita I wanted to paint, be an artist. She told me that what she really wanted was someone to love her, a house, and babies. And then she said nonchalantly to me, as she looked sideways at Georgette, "What do you know about that Navajo boy, the cowboy with the eyelashes, Clarence?" She had perfect timing, the mark of a good hunter or singer. She paused, then said, "He's a good kisser."

I hated confrontation and leaped back to get out of the way. "He's spoken for," choked Georgette, who stood up quickly to face her foe, spilling acetone all over Lupita and my favorite pants. The whole room stank of rotting apples.

Lupita knew exactly what Georgette had been up to all along when she'd invited her to our room. I wondered if she knew anything about Clarence's bet, and whether or not I should tell her. Lupita picked up Georgette's sharp nail file and pointed it at her before she began filing away.

Georgette wasn't through. "You Mexican bitch!" she snapped. "Get out of here."

"This is my room too," I added. "And she can stay. And by the way, please take off my pants."

Georgette glared at me as she quickly replaced my pants with her skirt. She kicked the ruined pants aside. "You're both sick," she snapped. "Nobody can be from Venus or anyplace else but here." She marched out of the room carrying her case of nail polish.

Later I made my way down the sidewalk to the painting studio to get myself back together. When I painted, everything else went away: the deals for seduction, the sad needs for attention, the missing fathers, fearful mothers, and evil stepfathers. I could fly to the moon, and to Venus, too, if I wanted. I understood Lupita when she said she was from Venus. I was from somewhere far away, the other side of the Milky Way, and would return there someday. I knew it, just as I knew I could count on cerulean blue to be absolutely cerulean blue when I spread it on the canvas.

The freeze from the approaching cold front fixed the stars to the dark sky perfectly in place. The powwow club was practicing in the gym, and a song flew out the tall narrow windows toward the white shell moon. The moon leaned delicately toward the bright planet of Venus, framed by the graceful cottonwoods lining the sidewalk. I felt flawed, imperfect, but what haunted me was not flamboyant like Georgette's ghost. It was a subtle thing, a graceful force even, like the field of stars my family saw in the night as we stomp-danced every summer. It was born of a kind of reason; that is, if there is such beauty, then why are we suffering here?

As I opened the door to the studio, Herbie jumped me. I screamed, then when I recognized him, we laughed. I chased him then held him down, made him promise never to frighten me again. Then I told him everything, about Lupita, about Georgette, about Mrs. Wilhelm and my stepfather, about the moon. He walked around me as I talked and got out my paints. He was high on possibilities, on hope and smoke.

"No!" I told him. "No, I can't," when he reminded me that he came over to take me to the dance at the canteen. "Today I made a promise to myself, and I can't risk getting sent home. And I need to paint." The incantations of the Doors wound through the campus and through the door of the studio, tempting me.

"You're running from yourself. You're hiding from reality. Let's go, let's face everything together. . . . Besides, I need you to check somebody for me. Aieeeeeee."

It was Lewis Jim. And when I thought of Lewis Jim, I remembered Lupita and the deal Clarence had going. Tonight was the deadline. I had to find Lupita and warn her before it was too late. She had plans to go to the dance.

The canteen was jammed. Herbie pulled me immediately out onto the dance floor. Dancing was like painting, like flying. Through rhythm I could travel toward the stars. Herbie and I could stay on the dance floor for hours, and if we stayed in the canteen and danced I couldn't drink or get into any other kind of trouble. While we danced, I kept my eyes on the door for Lupita. We danced every dance until a Mexican song interrupted, and all the Apache girls flooded the dance floor.

While they weaved back and forth, Herbie bought us Cokes and I looked around the room for Lupita. I didn't see her anywhere, or Clarence, either. Georgette stood outside, near the glass doors of the entrance. She looked small and alone as she borrowed a cigarette and lit it. I remembered the night she had upset the whole dorm with her panicked run from the ghost chasing her, and the big stink her roommates had caused when they demanded she move from their room. It wasn't just the ghost, they had charged; she was from an enemy tribe. No one had wanted a girl with a ghost in their rooms. I didn't want the

15

ghost either, but I felt sorry for the girl with the scratchy army blanket draped over her shoulders. The ghost had stayed away, but the fear kept following her.

I spotted Clarence coming up out of the dark, from the direction of the ditch. He was smiling and laughing too hard, walking with Lewis. Lupita wasn't with them. Clarence grabbed Georgette a little roughly. She smiled and melted into him, and then they came through the door and onto the dance floor, Lewis following behind them. Georgette beamed with her prize and made sure I saw her.

"Where's Lupita?" I demanded. A knot crawled up my stomach. Georgette glared at me.

"She's on Venus," said Clarence, and he and Lewis laughed. I didn't like the sound of their sly laughter.

I pulled a reluctant Herbie behind me. "We have to look for Lupita," I urged. He slid out the door of the packed canteen behind me.

"Wait, wait," he protested as he stared back at Lewis, who had no idea Herbie was interested in him. But Herbie was no fool. He knew better than to reveal his attraction as he pantomimed his broken heart behind Lewis's broad back.

We found Lupita almost immediately. "Over here," she called brightly. She waved us into the shadow between the painting and drawing studios. She was alone.

"Okay, Venus," joked Herbie. "This better be good. I just left the man of my dreams to come and look for you."

Her eyes shined as she pulled a pint of Everclear out

from under her jacket.

"You guys go ahead," I said. "I'll sit this one out." I was trying to be good. It was then I saw the rough smudge of dirt on Lupita's jacket, the dainty lace of twigs on her thick black hair, and the bruise decorating her wrist. I thought of Clarence and Lewis walking smugly into the dance. It was more than I could bear. I took a drink and then another.

I lost track of time. One minute we were all back in the canteen dancing in a line to "Cotton-Eyed Joe" and then the next we were sitting under the moon out near the ditch with a stranger from town we'd hired to make a run for us. The earth was spinning, and we were spinning with it. As we leaned into the burn, Lupita told us about her life, about how her mother had died when she was ten and left her with her father. She told how her father would tie her hair up every morning with her mother's ribbons before they left to work the fields together.

Herbie showed us the scar on his back made by a man who beat then raped him for his girlish ways. He made it sound funny, but I didn't laugh. I didn't say anything; I was numb and flying far away, listening to the whir of the story as it unwound beneath the glowing moon.

Herbie disappeared somewhere in the dark, and I could hear him throwing up. Someone was singing round dance songs. A dog barked from far, far away. Lupita had drifted into the bushes for what seemed years when the warning bell sounded from the girls' dorm. The sky was still spinning, but I willed myself to walk, step by step, to find Lupita, to make it back to the dorm in time. I looked for her through the blur of stars and sadness. I lost her. Without warning I remembered the stacked stones. I saw the unraveling story as it spun through time and space. And I saw what the old man had shown me that I hadn't been able to recall until now—how each thought and action fueled the momentum of the story—and how vulnerable we were to forgetting, all of us.

The final bell rang and I barely made it to my room, where I summoned a bit of soberness to save my life. I brushed my teeth so I would not smell like a drunk.

"Breathe," said the dorm assistant, whose job it was on Friday and Saturday nights to go to each room and smell each girl's breath for alcohol. She stood poised with her pen, ready to make a mark against my name. I admired her clean life. Her parents showed up every weekend to bring her chili and fresh bread. She always stayed on the safe side of rules. I breathed. Then breathed again easily when she marked me present and sober.

No one had seen Lupita. Georgette floated into the room. "By the way," she said coolly, "Mrs. Wilhelm is looking for you. She wants you to come to her office."

I was still drunk when I entered Mrs. Wilhelm's office, though I had learned to hide it well. Lupita was sobbing and falling apart in front of a stern and disappointed Mrs. Wilhelm. "I want to go home. I want to go back to Venus," she cried as she buried her face in her arms.

I had failed not once, but twice. I had failed to warn Lupita in time and I had failed the trust of Mrs. Wilhelm, who was the only person who had ever stood with me against the lies of my stepfather. Now Lupita would get sent home, not to Venus but to the father who had been sleeping with her since she was ten.

"Were you with Lupita tonight?" Mrs. Wilhelm sternly asked me.

What Mrs. Wilhelm was asking was whether or not I was drinking with Lupita. Immediately I thought of Georgette, the snitch. She had told. And maybe Mrs. Wilhelm didn't know, maybe she did. I couldn't tell for sure. But I knew that wasn't what really mattered. The truth became a path clearer than anything else, a shining luminescent bridge past all human failures. I could see the old man on the moon who always demanded nothing less than the truth. I had missed him, but he had returned, as he had promised.

I confessed. "Yes, I was with Lupita," and I knew terribly that I was most likely dooming myself back to the house of my stepfather.

"Go take care of Lupita," Mrs. Wilhelm said. "I will talk with the two of you tomorrow when you are sober." Then she slapped us each with a month of restriction. "I need you here, so I can keep a closer eye on you," she said.

I led the sodden Lupita back to her room. All night I held her while she cried for her mother, for home. All night, as we flew through the stars to the planet Venus.

Because My Father Always Said He Was the Only Indian Who Saw Jimi Hendrix Play "The Star-Spangled Banner" at Woodstock

SHERMAN ALEXIE

During the sixties, my father was the perfect hippie, since all the hippies were trying to be Indians. Because of that, how could anyone recognize that my father was trying to make a social statement?

But there is evidence, a photograph of my father demonstrating in Spokane, Washington, during the Vietnam War. The photograph made it onto the wire service and was reprinted in newspapers throughout the country. In fact, it was on the cover of *Time*.

In the photograph, my father is dressed in bell-bottoms and flowered shirt, his hair in braids, with red peace symbols splashed across his face like war paint. In his hands my father holds a rifle above his head, captured in that moment just before he proceeded to beat the shit out of the National Guard private lying prone on the ground. A fellow demonstrator holds a sign that is just barely visible over my father's left shoulder. It reads MAKE LOVE NOT WAR.

The photographer won a Pulitzer Prize, and editors across the country had a lot of fun creating captions and headlines. I've read many of them collected in my father's scrapbook, and my favorite was run in the *Seattle Times*. The caption under the photograph read DEMONSTRATOR GOES TO WAR FOR PEACE. The editors capitalized on my father's Native American identity with other headlines like ONE WARRIOR AGAINST WAR and PEACEFUL GATHERING TURNS INTO NATIVE UPRISING.

Anyway, my father was arrested and charged with attempted murder, which was reduced to assault with a deadly weapon. It was a high-profile case so my father was used as an example. Convicted and sentenced quickly, he spent two years in Walla Walla State Penitentiary. Although his prison sentence effectively kept him out of the war, my father went through a different kind of war behind bars.

"There was Indian gangs and white gangs and black gangs and Mexican gangs," he told me once. "And there was somebody new killed every day. We'd hear about somebody getting it in the shower or wherever and the word would go down the line. Just one word. Just the color of his skin. Red, white, black, or brown. Then we'd chalk it up on the mental scoreboard and wait for the next broadcast."

My father made it through all that, never got into any serious trouble, somehow avoided rape, and got out of prison just in time to hitchhike to Woodstock to watch Jimi Hendrix play "The Star-Spangled Banner."

"After all the shit I'd been through," my father said, "I figured Jimi must have known I was there in the crowd to play something like that. It was exactly how I felt."

Twenty years later, my father played his Jimi Hendrix tape until it wore down. Over and over, the house filled with the rockets' red glare and the bombs bursting in air. He'd sit by the stereo with a cooler of beer beside him and cry, laugh, call me over and hold me tight in his arms, his bad breath and body odor covering me like a blanket.

Jimi Hendrix and my father became drinking buddies. Jimi Hendrix waited for my father to come home after a long night of drinking. Here's how the ceremony worked:

1. I would lie awake all night and listen for the sounds of my father's pickup.
2. When I heard my father's pickup, I would run upstairs and throw Jimi's tape into the stereo.
3. Jimi would bend his guitar into the first note of "The Star-Spangled Banner" just as my father walked inside.
4. My father would weep, attempt to hum along with Jimi, and then pass out with his head on the kitchen table.
5. I would fall asleep under the table with my head near my father's feet.
6. We'd dream together until the sun came up.

The days after, my father would feel so guilty that he would tell me stories as a means of apology.

"I met your mother at a party in Spokane," my father told me once. "We were the only two Indians at the party. Maybe the only two Indians in the whole town. I thought she was so beautiful. I figured she was the kind of woman who could make buffalo walk on up to her and give up their lives. She wouldn't have needed to hunt. Every time we went walking, birds would follow us around. Hell, tumbleweeds would follow us around."

Somehow my father's memories of my mother grew more beautiful as their relationship became more hostile. By the time the divorce was final, my mother was quite possibly the most beautiful woman who ever lived.

"Your father was always half crazy," my mother told me more than once. "And the other half was on medication."

But she loved him, too, with a ferocity that eventually forced her to leave him. They fought each other with the kind of graceful anger that only love can create. Still, their love was passionate, unpredictable, and selfish. My mother and father would get drunk and leave parties abruptly to go home and make love.

"Don't tell your father I told you this," my mother said. "But there must have been a hundred times he passed out on top of me. We'd be right in the middle of it, he'd say *I love you*, his eyes would roll backwards, and then out went his lights. It sounds strange, I know, but those were good times."

I was conceived during one of those drunken nights,

half of me formed by my father's whiskey sperm, the other half formed by my mother's vodka egg. I was born a goofy reservation mixed drink, and my father needed me just as much as he needed every other kind of drink.

One night my father and I were driving home in a near-blizzard after a basketball game, listening to the radio. We didn't talk much. One, because my father didn't talk much when he was sober, and two, because Indians don't need to talk to communicate.

"Hello out there, folks, this is Big Bill Baggins, with the late-night classics show on KROC, 97.2 on your FM dial. We have a request from Betty in Tekoa. She wants to hear Jimi Hendrix's version of 'The Star-Spangled Banner' recorded live at Woodstock."

My father smiled, turned the volume up, and we rode down the highway while Jimi led the way like a snow-plow. Until that night, I'd always been neutral about Jimi Hendrix. But, in that near-blizzard with my father at the wheel, with the nervous silence caused by the dangerous roads and Jimi's guitar, there seemed to be more to all that music. The reverberation came to mean something, took form and function.

That song made me want to learn to play guitar, not because I wanted to be Jimi Hendrix and not because I thought I'd ever play for anyone. I just wanted to touch the strings, to hold the guitar tight against my body, invent a chord, and come closer to what Jimi knew, to what my father knew.

"You know," I said to my father after the song was

over, "my generation of Indian boys ain't ever had no real war to fight. The first Indians had Custer to fight. My great-grandfather had World War I, my grandfather had World War II, you had Vietnam. All I have is video games."

My father laughed for a long time, nearly drove off the road into the snowy fields.

"Shit," he said. "I don't know why you're feeling sorry for yourself because you ain't had to fight a war. You're lucky. Shit, all you had was that damn Desert Storm. Should have called it Dessert Storm because it just made the fat cats get fatter. It was all sugar and whipped cream with a cherry on top. And besides that, you didn't even have to fight it. All you lost during that war was sleep because you stayed up all night watching CNN."

We kept driving through the snow, talked about war and peace.

"That's all there is," my father said. "War and peace with nothing in between. It's always one or the other."

"You sound like a book," I said.

"Yeah, well, that's how it is. Just because it's in a book doesn't make it not true. And besides, why the hell would you want to fight a war for this country? It's been trying to kill Indians since the very beginning. Indians are pretty much born soldiers anyway. Don't need a uniform to prove it."

Those were the kinds of conversations that Jimi Hendrix forced us to have. I guess every song has a special meaning for someone somewhere. Elvis Presley is still showing up in 7-Eleven stores across the country, even though he's been dead for years, so I figure music just might be the most important thing there is. Music turned my father into a reservation philosopher. Music has powerful medicine.

"I remember the first time your mother and I danced," my father told me once. "We were in this cowboy bar. We were the only real cowboys there despite the fact that we're Indians. We danced to a Hank Williams song. Danced to that real sad one, you know. 'I'm So Lonesome I Could Cry.' Except your mother and I weren't lonesome or crying. We just shuffled along and fell right goddamn down into love."

"Hank Williams and Jimi Hendrix don't have much in common," I said.

"Hell, yes, they do. They knew all about broken hearts," my father said.

"You sound like a bad movie."

"Yeah, well, that's how it is. You kids today don't know shit about romance. Don't know shit about music either. Especially you Indian kids. You all have been spoiled by those drums. Been hearing them beat so long, you think that's all you need. Hell, son, even an Indian needs a piano or guitar or saxophone now and again."

My father played in a band in high school. He was the drummer. I guess he'd burned out on those. Now, he was like the universal defender of the guitar.

"I remember when your father would haul that old guitar out and play me songs," my mother said. "He couldn't play all that well but he tried. You could see him thinking about what chord he was going to play next. His eyes got all squeezed up and his face turned all red. He kind of looked that way when he kissed me, too. But don't tell him I said that."

Some nights I lay awake and listened to my parents' lovemaking. I know white people keep it quiet, pretend they don't ever make love. My white friends tell me they can't even imagine their own parents getting it on. I know exactly what it sounds like when my parents are touching each other. It makes up for knowing exactly what they sound like when they're fighting. Plus and minus. Add and subtract. It comes out just about even.

Some nights I would fall asleep to the sounds of my parents' lovemaking. I would dream Jimi Hendrix. I could see my father standing in the front row in the dark at Woodstock as Jimi Hendrix played "The Star-Spangled Banner." My mother was at home with me, both of us waiting for my father to find his way back home to the reservation. It's amazing to realize I was alive, breathing and wetting my bed, when Jimi was alive and breaking guitars.

I dreamed my father dancing with all these skinny hippie women, smoking a few joints, dropping acid, laughing when the rain fell. And it did rain there. I've seen actual news footage. I've seen the documentaries. It rained. People had to share food. People got sick. People got married. People cried all kinds of tears.

But as much as I dream about it, I don't have any clue about what it meant for my father to be the only Indian who saw Jimi Hendrix play at Woodstock. And maybe he wasn't the only Indian there. Most likely there were hundreds but my father thought he was the only one. He told me that a million times when he was drunk and a couple hundred times when he was sober.

"I was there," he said. "You got to remember this was near the end and there weren't as many people as before. Not nearly as many. But I waited it out. I waited for Jimi."

A few years back, my father packed up the family and the three of us drove to Seattle to visit Jimi Hendrix's grave. We had our photograph taken lying down next to the grave. There isn't a gravestone there. Just one of those flat markers.

Jimi was twenty-eight when he died. That's younger than Jesus Christ when he died. Younger than my father as we stood over the grave.

"Only the good die young," my father said.

"No," my mother said. "Only the crazy people choke to death on their own vomit."

"Why you talking about my hero that way?" my father asked.

"Shit," my mother said. "Old Jesse WildShoe choked to death on his own vomit and he ain't anybody's hero."

I stood back and watched my parents argue. I was used to these battles. When an Indian marriage starts to fall apart, it's even more destructive and painful than usual. A hundred years ago, an Indian marriage was broken easily. The woman or man just packed up all their possessions and left the tipi. There were no arguments, no discussions.

Now, Indians fight their way to the end, holding onto the last good thing, because our whole lives have to do with survival.

After a while, after too much fighting and too many angry words had been exchanged, my father went out and bought a motorcycle. A big bike. He left the house often to ride that thing for hours, sometimes for days. He even strapped an old cassette player to the gas tank so he could listen to music. With that bike, he learned something new about running away. He stopped talking as much, stopped drinking as much. He didn't do much of anything except ride that bike and listen to music.

Then one night my father wrecked his bike on Devil's Gap Road and ended up in the hospital for two months. He broke both his legs, cracked his ribs, and punctured a lung. He also lacerated his kidney. The doctors said he could have died easily. In fact, they were surprised he made it through surgery, let alone survived those first few hours when he lay on the road, bleeding. But I wasn't surprised. That's how my father was.

And even though my mother didn't want to be married to him anymore and his wreck didn't change her mind about that, she still came to see him every day. She sang Indian tunes under her breath, in time with the hum of the machines hooked into my father. Although my father could barely move, he tapped his finger in rhythm.

When he had the strength to finally sit up and talk, hold conversations, and tell stories, he called for me.

"Victor," he said. "Stick with four wheels."

After he began to recover, my mother stopped visiting as often. She helped him through the worst, though. When he didn't need her anymore, she went back to the life she had created. She traveled to powwows, started to dance again. She was a champion traditional dancer when she was younger.

"I remember your mother when she was the best traditional dancer in the world," my father said. "Everyone wanted to call her sweetheart. But she only danced for me. That's how it was. She told me that every other step was just for me."

"But that's only half of the dance," I said.

"Yeah," my father said. "She was keeping the rest for herself. Nobody can give everything away. It ain't healthy."

"You know," I said, "sometimes you sound like you ain't even real."

"What's real? I ain't interested in what's real. I'm interested in how things should be."

My father's mind always worked that way. If you don't like the things you remember, then all you have to do is change the memories. Instead of remembering the bad things, remember what happened immediately before. That's what I learned from my father. For me, I remember how good the first drink of that Diet Pepsi tasted instead of how my mouth felt when I swallowed a wasp with the second drink.

Because of all that, my father always remembered the second before my mother left him for good and took me with her. No. I remembered the second before my father left my mother and me. No. My mother remembered the second before my father left her to finish raising me all by herself.

But however memory actually worked, it was my father who climbed on his motorcycle, waved to me as I stood in the window, and rode away. He lived in Seattle, San Francisco, Los Angeles, before he finally ended up in Phoenix. For a while, I got postcards nearly every week. Then it was once a month. Then it was on Christmas and my birthday.

On a reservation, Indian men who abandon their children are treated worse than white fathers who do the same thing. It's because white men have been doing that forever and Indian men have just learned how. That's how assimilation can work.

My mother did her best to explain it all to me, although I understood most of what happened.

"Was it because of Jimi Hendrix?" I asked her.

"Part of it, yeah," she said. "This might be the only marriage broken up by a dead guitar player."

"There's a first time for everything, enit?"

"I guess. Your father just likes being alone more than he likes being with other people. Even me and you."

Sometimes I caught my mother digging through old photo albums or staring at the wall or out the window. She'd get that look on her face that I knew meant she missed my father. Not enough to want him back. She missed him just enough for it to hurt.

On those nights I missed him most I listened to music.

31

Not always Jimi Hendrix. Usually I listened to the blues. Robert Johnson mostly. The first time I heard Robert Johnson sing I knew he understood what it meant to be Indian on the edge of the twenty-first century, even if he was black at the beginning of the twentieth. That must have been how my father felt when he heard Jimi Hendrix. When he stood there in the rain at Woodstock.

Then on the night I missed my father most, when I lay in bed and cried, with that photograph of him beating that National Guard private in my hands, I imagined his motorcycle pulling up outside. I knew I was dreaming it all but I let it be real for a moment.

"Victor," my father yelled. "Let's go for a ride."

"I'll be right down. I need to get my coat on."

I rushed around the house, pulled my shoes and socks on, struggled into my coat, and ran outside to find an empty driveway. It was so quiet, a reservation kind of quiet, where you can hear somebody drinking whiskey on the rocks three miles away. I stood on the porch and waited until my mother came outside.

"Come on back inside," she said. "It's cold."

"No," I said. "I know he's coming back tonight."

My mother didn't say anything. She just wrapped me in her favorite quilt and went back to sleep. I stood on the porch all night long and imagined I heard motorcycles and guitars, until the sun rose so bright that I knew it was time to go back inside to my mother. She made breakfast for both of us and we ate until we were full.

A Real-Live Blond Cherokee and His
Equally Annoyed Soul Mate

CYNTHIA LEITICH SMITH

I'm a swear-to-God, card-carrying, respectably thick blood Oklahoma Cherokee. That's right, I said "Cherokee." And yeah, my hair is blond. Sandy blond.

Sure, I know every "take-me-to-your-sweat-lodge" wannabe claims he's a Cherokee. Yeah, Mama's mama is the full blood. No, I didn't call her a "princess," and don't make fun of my gramma. So what if I'm not dark like her or a redhead like Dad's mama? I took after my grandpas, the Swedes.

Really. Check out this picture in my wallet. It's from my cousin Robbie's wedding last spring. Here's my tribal ID. And if you're wondering how my family got to Austin, Texas—well, we drove a U-Haul truck south down I-35.

That's all right, nothing personal. But now, you understand.

Looks aside, I'm a real-live Indian, and I felt like one

when Little Miss Gentrification tapped my shoulder at work and said in this whooshy breath, "Mickey tells me that you're part Native American. My American history teacher, Mr. Cavazos, he says that we have to use primary sources because if you want to find out about a people's history, you have to hear their side. As it turns out, I'm getting a C minus in history, and I was wondering if I could interview you about—"

"No," I replied, hanging the frayed, oversized clown pants back up. I worked at this funky costume shop on South Congress called All The World's A Stage. Clown pants were on the pedestrian side of our collection.

It took the girl a second to recover, and I remembered seeing her earlier that day. She'd walked into the shop, flipped through the wands, swords, and umbrellas section, taken one look at me, and fled. As I checked the mesh skirt on a ballet tutu, she began again, "But Mickey said—"

"Mickey," I clarified, "is my boss. My heritage is not work related." I strode past her through a maze of stuffed clothes hangers to the stacks of magician and *The Cat in the Hat*–style hats.

She was harmless. Mildly offensive, definitely intrusive, but no different from a thousand other spoiled teenage girls when it came to things like Indian identity or, say, the fact that she was sporting dyed red hair, a gauzy green dress, two nose rings, and an infinity tattoo, which, in this neighborhood, made her a walking cliché.

The bell over the front door jangled, and the girl who'd been talking to me was gone. That's that, I figured.

Easy come, easy . . . You know, she had these green eyes. They reminded me of someone else's eyes. While helping a frantic indie filmmaker pick out three parasols and six pairs of white elbow gloves, I tried to remember whose.

A half hour or so later, a trio of very frat-looking guys cruised in.

"Can I help y'all?" I asked. Hey, it was my job.

One of them held up a hand, dismissing me. "In a minute, man."

I strolled from the makeup display past a row of soft rubber head masks to take my station behind a glass counter case filled with plastic and rhinestone jewelry. Then I glanced around the store, watching the college guys pore through the racks of costumes.

Their behavior was textbook. Some guffaws at the classic horror capes, the Dracula and/or Frankenstein impression, a repeated joke or two from the latest slasher flick, and a jeering gibe at the most beta of their pack, daring him to rent a showgirl feather boa. I checked the time on my runner's watch, already bored.

Just then, one of the college guys pulled out a Wild West Indian costume. It was ugly, cheap, and ridiculous looking—suede fringe and purple feathers on the obligatory psuedo-Plains headdress. He held the costume up to himself, and—as if all that wasn't enough—started making "war whoops."

The costume must be new for Halloween, I thought, gripping the edge of the glass counter until it cut into my palms. "Mickey!" I called, but nobody answered. He'd already taken off for lunch.

Maybe the minstrel show of an Indian costume was no big deal, not by itself. But it was one of a million little things (not to mention a few biggies), and they just kept on coming . . . like everybody who didn't believe in blond Cherokees . . . like a pretty but stupid girl who thought I was exotic. You know, I didn't even get her name.

Mine is Jason, like that "Friday the 13th" hockey mask on the shelf between the rubber skull and the Hillary Clinton face.

When the Indian costume landed on my glass counter, I was thinking about how much I needed that summer job. Even though the dot-commers were now all unemployed, they'd already driven up the cost of living near downtown. My dad wasn't high up at Dell. He was replaceable, and more recently, underemployed. Mama had her hands full at home with my baby brothers, the twins.

I was so busy mulling this over that I didn't hear the front doorbell and I didn't notice that Miss Gentrification had returned . . . at least not until she slammed her paper cup of cranberry tea on the glass counter in front of me. A tiny bit splashed out onto the, God, *purple* fake Indian feathers, and I offered her my first smile of the day.

When I looked into those iced evergreen eyes, they were furious and a little teary. My fault, I realized, dropping my gaze to the amulet she wore around her neck. It was some kind of female power symbol, a little more mystic than you'd find at the neighborhood herb store.

Her hand was still wrapped around the paper cup.

"I didn't come in here," she began, "to get your help with my report."

That was interesting.

"I'm not getting a C minus in history. A person could be in a coma in Mr. Cavazos's class and still pull a straight C."

She lied. I didn't like liars.

"The truth is that I came in here to ask you out, and I've never asked out a guy before, and I needed an excuse to talk to you. I'm not really good with guys."

I forgave her.

"But now, of course, since you're such a hugely unfriendly, mean, horrible, evil person, I just want to let you know that I have lost absolutely all interest." Before I could get a thought together, she'd spun in her wood sandals and headed toward the door, taking her tea with her.

"Wait!" I called, trying to think of something more to say.

"Nika!" shouted the war-whooping guy from the back of the store.

She stopped with her hand on the doorknob. But not for me. For him.

"Chad!" she replied.

Chad left his friends, made his way to the front of the store, and hugged . . . what was her name? Nika.

"Hey, *dude*," Chad called back to one of his pals, "pay for my costume, all right? I'll get the keg and meet you back at the house." Then he wrapped a beefy arm around Nika and walked out of my costume shop with her.

Jeez. I couldn't figure out how a quirky urban princess like that would even know . . . whatever he was. The Chad. And to boot, I had to spend the next five minutes ringing up his friends, who'd picked up such exciting, original costumes as the villain from the *Scream* series, George W, and an emergency room MD.

As they finally jostled out of the front door, Mickey strolled in from the back. He was smiling and whistling. He'd gotten some *queso* on his prized T-shirt that read "Note Vader" on one side and "Vote Nader" on the other.

"Back from lunch," he said. "Did I miss anythin'?"

At one-fifteen, I rang up Jack and Jill and figured that fate was just like that.

At two o'clock, I helped Liza straighten his wig and decided that any girl who'd want Chad wasn't good enough for me.

At three-nineteen, I watched Sonny and Cher leave hand in hand and worried that Chad was five or six years older than Nika.

At three forty-one, the entire command crew of the *Enterprise* (original series) needed new communicators, and I realized it was no big deal.

At four-eleven, I looked into a crystal ball and it was clear that I should've been dating Indian girls anyway.

At five-thirty, Catwoman salsa-danced in the aisles with Scooby Doo, and I remembered that Mickey was the one who told Nika about me. I realized that he might know how I could get in contact with her.

At six o'clock, Mickey explained that Nika's family

had started attending his Unitarian church last week, and that he'd invited them to stop by and check out the shop. Nice folks, he said. Lived by the microwave tower in Clarksville. Then he announced that we needed to do a little last-minute inventory before the Halloween rush. I spent excruciating minutes counting things like wax fangs, pirate hoop earrings, and the blow-up sheep belonging to Ms. Peep.

It still didn't get dark early yet, not in mid-October. I could see the smoke long before I found the house. It was a two-bedroom stone cottage in the hilly historic Clarksville neighborhood, and the front faced one of those long, steep alleys. To get there, I had to jog the hike-and-bike trail alongside downtown and cross the lake via the new pedestrian bridge. When I arrived, the temperature was still in the eighties, and sweat was pouring down my back and neck.

Ahead, the smoke billowed darker, denser.

Call me bold. Call me a trespasser. Call me an idiot. But I let myself into the gate and found Nika perched on a garden bench not far from a metal garbage can. I could see a low flame flickering out of the top. Leaves, I figured, burning leaves.

"Hi," I said, feeling daring. I considered mentioning that leaf burning was probably in violation of some city ordinance, but it wasn't really the kind of line I wanted to open with. I'd believed her when she confessed to being bad with guys. The truth was that I wasn't much of an expert with girls, either.

Nika had changed out of her quirky urban princess ensemble. She was wearing a plain white T-shirt and cut-off jeans. She didn't bother replying, but she didn't ask me to leave, either. For a while, we sat quietly side by side on the bench.

This is stupid, I thought. She's a mildly offensive, definitely intrusive, spoiled . . . It didn't matter. I'd sought her out. I'd run to get there. But I still really hated Chad.

"He's my brother," she explained, even though I hadn't asked the question.

I was relieved and disappointed all at once.

"He's always good to me . . . kind of overprotective . . . sort of annoying. But good." Her tone was apologetic.

I glanced at her hair and realized it wasn't dyed red; it was natural. My gaze followed the blazing hue up to the flames from the garbage can a few feet away. The color wasn't quite the same; her hair was a deeper red, more alive. Staring more carefully at the small blaze, I realized that what was burning wasn't leaves.

It was fake Indian fringe and fake Indian feathers. Some of them were purple. She'd torched the costume that her brother Chad had rented from my store.

Nika said, "I'll pay Mickey back."

I rubbed my eyes. "It's the smoke," I explained, surprised by how much the gesture affected me. Glad that somebody else got it for once, that it wasn't up to me to deal alone. I understood now why I'd had to find her.

When I looked back down at Nika again, I saw hints

of my grandmother. Not my Cherokee grandma, my Irish one. The one with those eyes people sing about on street corners and in late-night bars. The one who was annoyed by the Celtic fad and framed four-leaf clovers. The one who couldn't stand the folks who flocked to see *Lord of the Dance*. Wannabes, Gramma called them. Gramma with her iced evergreen eyes.

Nika straightened, pulling her knees to her chest. "I'm thinking of taking up Wicca," she said, "and not just because it's almost Halloween."

My hand moved as if I had no control over it, and my fingers gently threaded her crimson locks. Lots of people were as inclined to burn witches these days as those townsfolk back in old Salem. I guessed I knew how that felt. The fact that times were better didn't mean they couldn't still be bad. Besides, I was okay with witches, at least the Wiccan kind.

I ran my palm down the curve of her freckled cheek to her chin, and I lifted it gently. At least she had the witchy looks for it, I thought, the classic coloring.

The Last Snow of the Virgin Mary

RICHARD VAN CAMP

My name is Kevin Garner and I keep telling myself that dealing isn't who I am. It's not who I want to be. Sure, I make great money, but I run the risk of being busted. And check this out: There are three joints to a gram—ten bucks a joint or thirty bucks a gram. An eighth is three and a half grams. A quarter is five, six, or seven grams, depending if you eye it up or weigh it, and depending on if you're dealing with a frequent flyer. If you don't have your weights and you're making a deal on the spot, a Loonie weighs seven grams. A half ounce—we're talking dry, fluffy pot here—is two to three fingers. An ounce is four. For wet, stinky, clingy pot—never measure with your fingers, as seven grams can look like three. There are always twenty-eight grams on the ounce: thirty bucks a pop. You make 840 bucks if you're not smokin' or spending. A half-ounce is fourteen grams. There are sixteen ounces to a pound, eight ounces to a half-pound, and four ounces to a quarter pound. A pound, or an elbow, you can buy for $3,500 or $4,000, depending on the quality, the grade of the smoke, and who you're dealing with. There are 448 grams in a pound. You can make $13,000 minimum on a pound if you sell it by the gram. There are some like Joey who can make 4,600 joints from a single pound—I'm not there yet, but I'm working on it.

Right now I got the sniffles and I need my vitamins. A Cocoa Puff would be nice. I'm sitting at the control deck monitoring the controls. Got six smokes left, some ginseng tea. My nose is still dripping from the cold of the arena, but I am pleased. The game was a success. Lots of slashing, high-sticking, and cross-checking to keep the sheep happy. Hockey's just a modern-day lacrosse. How come nobody at Hockey Night in Canada talks about that? I'm surprised Don Cherry doesn't just say, "It's just a matter of time, folks, before players are allowed to kill one another for public spectacle, so just hang in there, eh!"

The first few goals usually tell the tale, but the Spruce Kings lost to Fort Smith. I, nonetheless, shined brighter than a thousand suns. Man, she was cold at the rink.

Torque. Sandy's physics final exam's tomorrow, and the kid's stuck on torque. The little guy reminds me of myself when I was that age, and I'm doing my best to nurture and foster. Now torque, as I explained when I was tutoring him, is the physics of twisting and turning about an axis measured in Newton meters. Christ, I hope he gets it.

The hardcore party crowd still doesn't believe I'm trying to change, that I'm serious about declaring the trailer off-limits. I had to run to the trailer, get my old VCR tapes beside the porn and WWF archives, and lock the doors. That Love Shack of mine is trouble, and I have to lose it. If I'm going to be a teacher, I have to have a place to study, and if I'm gonna get Lona, I have to prove to her I can change. Leo's not too happy I'm quitting either, and I really gotta think about this. I owe him six grand, and I got nothing to show for it. I've been evading his phone calls, even his drive-by's. He was the one who spoiled me, shouldn't have given me that kind of freedom. I was the only dealer in town who didn't pay deposits on the fronts cuz I had the high school crowd. I saved my best for the regulars, saved the bad for the young-dumb-and-full-of-cums. They didn't know the difference and, really, what were they gonna say? Who were they gonna tell?

This hockey game means everything. Can't blow it. I got a pound in my packsack, my last ounce on the street. I'm selling out today. All of it. I'm really trying to change. I'm tutoring, laying off the dope and the booze. I've had mine, but it's time to move on. I just gotta be a teacher. Taping and broadcasting this game is my ticket out. When my alarm clock rings in the morning, it might as well be a bugle: I am on a mission and the only thing that's gonna stop me is a bullet from an elephant gun.

Eleven this morning, head pounding, I headed to the college to finally get the application forms and who do I see? Goddamn stuck in the eighties Shari with her bangs reaching for the moon. Everybody calls her Skull Face cuz you can already tell what her skull looks like.

"Whatcha here for, Kev?" Shari asked. She's the receptionist at the college.

God, I was hung over. "Application for the Teacher Education Program."

"Sha right!"

I couldn't stop staring at her lemming teeth stuffed into a Caesarean smile. "Seriously."

"You want to be a teacher?"

It hits me I haven't shaved. Good thing I'm gorgeous. "I want to be a teacher."

"How old are you?"

"Eighteen."

"You, Kevin Garner, want to teach kids?"

I massaged my temples with my thumbs. "Can you be funny later and just give me the application forms?"

"You want parents to trust their kids with you? Your truck's still parked outside the bar and you're here registering for the Teacher Education Program."

Ah, I thought, every Welfare Wednesday for the rest of your forgettable life, you're gonna be dancing to the same tunes at the Legion while I'm down south teaching.

"You're gonna have to cut your hair, you know," she said as she went to get the application. Someone tapped me on the shoulder. It was Mr. Chang, the richest man in town. Also Chinese. He was holding an invoice in his hand. While everybody else in town owed Mr. Chang money, I was one of the proud few who didn't. My overhead's low, so I got satellite. I got no use for "Friends" and, really, they should tape the next "Survivor" up here cuz no one would make it, no one at all.

"You want to be teacher?" he asked.

"Yeah, Mr. Chang." I wiped my nose with my sleeve. "I really do."

"How come you never told me that before?" he asked.

"I just figured it out this year," I said.

My auntie who abandoned me and moved to Hay River after Grandma passed made him his parka. She owed him eight hundred bucks for an overdue cable bill. No problem. She made the parka for him and they called it even. Just like that.

"Good decision, school," he said. "Good money. Summers off. Get to see the world. Help the kids." He studied me for a bit before he said anything more. I had sold his son a few grams, and maybe he knew it. "You want another job?" he asked.

I thought about it. Me? I thought, Wait a minute. Use this. Earn the town's trust. Pay Leo off. Impress Lona and set her free. Let the town see what you can do and become a teacher. I smiled and said, "Sure."

"Hockey game finals are tonight at eight. Everybody wants to watch. Hay River, Smith, Yellowknife, and Simpson. I need someone to tape the game and play it for the communities after. You do this. I write you a letter. You get into TEP, I bet."

Mr. Chang was right. Not only was I Dogrib, he knew with my past I'd never get into the program. I figured if

46

people found out I did all the tape recording tonight and coordinated the broadcasting of the hockey game from the Cable TV station, surely someone at Aurora College . . . and Lona . . . and Leo . . . and Sandy . . . and that pig Morris—would all see I was trying to change my ways.

"So when's the next bash at your trailer?" Shari asked.

"Never again," I said. "I'm finished."

"Wah!" she said. "Get out of here."

I looked at Mr. Chang, who smiled and gave me the coolest nod ever. "Let's go get the equipment," he said.

I got the camcorder from Cable TV and got a quick how-to, but I already knew how. I had taped and broadcast the talent show for the past three years, so it was no prob. I had helped Mr. Chang hook up the video feed the summer before at the college so the students here could have videoconferencing with other students and instructors across Canada and the north, so he knew I was good to go. I stumbled past my parked truck (where are my keys?) outside the Terminal and ran all the way home before running to school to start tutoring. The snow's been cheap this winter. Ski-Dooers are mad. Everyone's got new machines, but no snow to drive on.

Mr. Chang gave me twenty bucks for new videotapes, but I pocketed it. That twenty would cover my application fee for college housing. I figured I could record over some tapes I had in my trailer. I dialed my answering machine from the TV station and hit my password: 6969. Five messages. Better not be five scores waiting to happen. Sat down. Gathered my vitamins out of my packsack.

47

Pressed play as I gathered my Excaliburs: two saw blades wrapped with electrical tape. Those were my buddies, red-hot right away and perfect for hot knifing.

"Kev, Jazz here. How's your elbow? Doctor says for thirty-five hundred he'll look at it. This Sunday at the Chinese Smorg. Ciao, bro. Don't spank it too hard or you'll get a purple head!" *Click!*

Sakes! I wrote this down. I told him not to use the phone. I told him to use the "Saturday Night Request Show" tonight. Send out a request to me. I get back to him from the pay phone downtown. An elbow equals an lb.—a pound. Thirty-five hundred for the quality I got. Why not? There's my tuition and then some. Do they really have a Badger on my line? I popped 1,000 mg's of vitamin C, 800 I.U.'s of vitamin E, 250 mcg's of vitamin B12, 1,000 mg's of Imperial Dragon Korean Red Ginseng, and two Kyolic Garlics. Guzzled it all down with my last cold Canadian.

Next message.

"Kev, Larry here. What are you burning? Three spot a G spot or what? Gimme call, you. Stay hard." *Click!*

I shook my head. Translation from Larry's Raven Talk: Can you please lend me three dollars so I can take you out for coffee, but I won't have to pay you back because, after all, I took you out for coffee, hozer."

Big burp. One last blast with the Excaliburs. No. Not in here. Not in the station. Oh, hell. Truly, hot knifing's where it's at: quick, efficient, no smoke wasted. This would be my thirty-third hot knife off the same gram.

Right arm, right arm. Doesn't 90 percent of digestion take place in the mouth?

I've been stoned since I was sixteen. Back then it was like get stoned, see what happens. Now it's like make money off people getting stoned and make things happen. I'm paying for it, though. How are my fingers? I have started to notice lately that I feel like I'm missing fingers. I believe the end plates of my nerves are rusting with THC, and my left eye clicks whenever I roll it backward. The enzymes in my blood that fuel my dreams are working overtime, and my arms fall asleep quicker than normal. When they tingle, does that mean they're dreaming? The dope's finally starting to catch up with me. I noticed a long time ago that those who start smoking up during their growth spurt develop retarded. They can't do small things with their fingers as they get older. They get lazy, lack hope. I started hooting after growing six foot even, so I'm okay—or I was. Now I get déjà vu's all the time and I'm starting to dream: not dream dream, but *dream* like the old-timers. Spooky.

Next message. Lona? Pleeaaassssse . . .

"Kev, this is Leo. Listen, it's a good day for a ride. We need to talk—"

Fast forward. Sorry, boss. Next. *Beep.* Lona? Nothing. Then—

"Kevin. This is Constable Morris Spencer here. Just wanted to see if you thought any more about our talk. You can call me here at the detachment. Talk to you soon." *Click!*

The hell with you, Morris. Good thing no one was here. They'd think I was turning narc. It was this goddamn cop that was making me change my ways. Morris took me to the cop shop, poured me a coffee I couldn't taste, and told me this was just a talk between "Skins" (yeah, right, pig!). Then the bastard took out the infamous Black Book that the cops keep denying they have. "Kevin," he said, "you know what this is and your name's in it. You're a young man; you don't have a record. We know you've moved a lot of dope for Leo. This is your only warning. I want you to get out of the racket, Kev. Think about it. If there's something you'd rather be doing, you better start doing it now."

"Can I go now?" I asked. What else could I say?

"Can you go now?" He took off his glasses, pressed his fingers into the side pockets of his tired eyes, and had a look at what had oozed there all day before wiping it on his pants. "Do you know what a Badger is, Kevin? It's a neat little computer program we have. It shows who Leo calls, and he calls you a lot, doesn't he? It shows who you call. It just grows and grows. We find out a whole network every time you make a call or someone calls you. Neat, eh? It looks like a spiderweb, and when we prepare it for evidence it makes search warrants really easy, especially in this town. We've already looked into your bank account, Kevin. How did you pay off your trailer so fast?"

About a thousand small heart attacks later, I lied, "Inheritance, okay? My grandma died. Can I go now? Got places to be, know what I mean?"

No calls from Lona. I get ass cramps just thinking about her. *The Fort Simmer Journal* did this article on her and talked about how a modeling agency flew her to Edmonton and took her pictures and has already started lining up deals for her. The town calls her "the little Shania Twain" because she's only five foot six, but what a body. A total knockout. I can't believe she hasn't seen through Dean yet, and I kept hinting about that when we talked at the party. The hell with Dean. Is it just wishful thinking or are they drifting? She's always eyeing me up at the bush parties. Cousin or no, what can Dean give her? That yellow-toothed loser. He lives on top of the bar, for Christ sakes.

I don't give a damn if he knows Lona and I lay together and talked well past midnight—before I scared her away.

Man, what a one-nipple town. I watch the monitor. It's just about halftime in my broadcasting of the game here at the studio, and I can't believe what Black Fonzy said back at the rink.

The Fort Simmer Spruce Kings ran like crippled trees from their dressing room. Their jerseys are white and black. The team was hung over. You could smell it. Wanna whiff? Think of snails in the same shoebox for a month; now multiply that by sixty-nine.

When the Spruce Kings got to the ice, they kicked off their skate guards and pushed themselves away.

Black Fonzy. What a burnout. "Yo, Kev!" he said as he chopped past me on his skates. "Leo's been lookin' for you."

I changed the battery for the camera. "Leo? Yeah yeah. We met."

"You met? He was just here."

What a burnout. "Yeah, we met."

"Oh." He looked around. "Think you can score me any more of that Jamaican finger hash?"

Black Fonzy was center for Simmer, also Skull Face's old man. Players call him Black Fonzy because he's Slavey and he's a darky. They also call him the Fist of God cuz if he checks you, you'll come to about a hundred feet up looking down on your own body. "Naw, man. I quit."

Fonzy's nose bull's-eyed his dopey face. "You're turning narc on us, or what?"

"I want to get into the TEP program."

"That's funny." He laughed. "You teach? I heard Leo's got some chocolate-covered 'shrooms. Why don't you score us some and I'll split it. I got fifty."

"I'm serious, man. I quit."

"Gonna join the robots, huh? What about your weights and torch?"

"You can have them for eighty."

"Fifty."

"Seventy-five."

"Sixty."

"Done."

"What about the trailer that cold hard hash made?"

"Sellin' it," I told him.

"I can't see this happening," he said, and skated away.

"Sheep," I whispered.

That was when the grunge casualty shuffled up to me, looking this way, that way.

"Mr. Garner?"

Some kid. I couldn't remember his name. His hair was so greasy it looked like he combed bear grease into his mop. Behind him, a Mongolian horde of snowboarders and shithead skaters posed strong.

"Can you sell me a bag?" he asked.

"A bag of what?" I looked around. "Chips? How old are you?"

"We got cash."

I looked around expecting to see that pig Morris watching us. "Get out of here," I said. "Go."

He blushed, shrugged, shambled off back toward the stands, and swore.

Decomposers everywhere . . .

"All right, lay-deeeees and gentlemen," I say clearly again as I track the players, "Welcome to Moccasin Square Gardens. Tonight I, Kevin Garner, am your play-by-play emcee as Fort Simmer tries to down Yellowknife for the territorial championships. . . ."

I follow the game and crack the best jokes I know. This hangover means nothing. It all rests on tonight. God, I feel it. I'm speaking to the communities, but I'm really speaking to Lona, Leo, and Constable Morris.

The game: I cracked a slew of jokes. I talked with the crowd between periods, and asked Sandy what he thought of the game.

"Simmer blew a two-goal lead!" he yelled. It wasn't

what I was looking for so I asked, "What's your greatest joy these days in our little community?"

The little champ looked right into the camera and said, "You, Mister Garner! You're the best tutor I've ever had!"

Bingo. The money shot. I swear to God everyone around me clapped. Man, I hope the college president caught that.

The phone rang at the cable station. My palms started burning, just like my grandma's when she knew something huge was going to happen.

It was Lona!

"You're amazing, Kevin!" she said. "Keep up the great work. This is a great hockey game. I'm sorry for what I said Friday night." My little Shania Twain. Brothers of the world, there is a God and His name is love! Maybe in heaven the guitar solos never end and you get the chick you've always wanted.

"Lona," I said. "Thanks for calling." I was feeling so high and so cocky from the game, but I knew I had to ask: "Hey, did you listen to that tape I made you? That first song, it's called 'Smothered Hope' by Skinny Puppy. Beautiful, hey? That's the remix off their *Dystemper* album. It's rare and precious, is what I'm trying to say. Like you. I put the Ministry's remix of it on side B, but I like this one the best—"

"Kevin, we shouldn't be talking."

I took a puff. "Why?"

"You and Dean are cousins. I don't want to cause friction."

My heart had a G spot right then and there. I had to sit down. There was hope. I blew my nose. "Are you two still going out?"

"He's trying, Kevin."

"Trying?" I stood up. "He's on the road for Leo. That's not trying. We just have to dance once, baby, you and me. I got some new moves that'll make you blush, all the moves you can handle."

"Kevin—"

"Listen." I took another puff. "I'm gonna be a teacher, you know, and I'm out of the dealing business as of tonight. Lona, you're the one for me. I swear to God. I'm sorry I scared you at the party. I'm dying to taste you—"

"I should get going."

"What? What'd I say? Look. I want to kiss you. Look, can I kiss you?"

"What did Dean do to my back?" she asks, and I can tell she's been wanting to ask me this since Friday.

"I don't want to scare you, so I'm not going to tell you. I got a plan anyways, so don't worry about it."

"You're stoned," she said. "I can tell. Good-bye."

What? The phone rang again. "Lona?"

Someone was laughing. Music was playing. I could hear the hockey game. My hockey game. I had Dolby Surround Sound of my hockey game. "Kevin?" a voice giggled. "Kevin? This is Aleaha Apples. Come over. We're in room three-oh-four. Women's residence. Bring all your dope."

I sat up. "Who is this?"

55

"Aleaha Apples. We heard you're selling your stash, and we'll buy you out."

"Who told you this?"

"Black Fonzy."

The word was out now. "Who's all there?"

"Us. Come soon." She burst out laughing and hung up.

Hmmm. If I sell out, I'm free. Maybe pay what I make to Leo . . . or hit the road with Lona.

On the last tape now at Cable TV. Soon the footage will come. Soon. The twenty that Mr. Chang gave me turned out handy. Ordered pizza. She's on the way. Forget the student residence fees for a while. I am celebrating.

Nineteen minutes left on the last tape, and Yellowknife, Hay River, Smith, and Fort Simpson are watching. Tomorrow, when I go for a coffee uptown, everyone's gonna know my name.

Last Friday. After the party. With Lona. Lying down with her on my bed. Had a good cry about my grandmother being gone. She wiped away my tears and kissed my neck. She was the first person I ever told about holding my grandmother's hand for five days before she died. I slid my hands up her shirt but stayed away from the goods. No way. Slow down, I thought. *Earn her.* Her strong, smooth back. She unbuttoned my shirt and ran her hands over me. We were flush faced and shivering, and I was starting to breathe heavy, heavier than her. I told her how I was at the crossroads, how anything could happen. I wasn't so far gone that I couldn't turn it all around. I told her about a teacher I had, Mrs. Stellan. I was thinking

56

about how she always believed in me and, man, when you have that, anything's possible. I was telling her I'd like to be that somebody for those without, and I can empathize.

I then told her about my ability of echolocation.

"What?"

"I lie on my bed, turn the music off, and send my psychic lasso your way. I know where you were Tuesday night."

She smiled. "Okay. Where?"

"The café. You had a coffee and fries with gravy on the side. You then ordered iced tea with a twist of lemon for dessert."

Her eyes lit up. "Where was I Wednesday?"

"Your house helping your mom bake bread. You thought about me all day."

Her jaw dropped. "How did you—"

I smiled. "Echolocation. Like bats. I send out my psychic feelers. When I was a kid, I used to walk on the tops of the trees outside the house when I dreamed. Now I just send the signals out there, like a slow spell, and I reel it in. My grandma had medicine. Maybe she passed it on to me."

She kissed my forehead. "You're crazy."

I played the mix I made for her. Whitesnake played "Still of the Night" and it got to the solo where the violins play together, like bees dancing, and I always get the shivers when I hear it. As more violins escalate, I feel like I'm climbing the northern lights with a peace stronger than Prozac, and I want to lick something and put my fist through glass at the same time.

I never should have told her about my dream.

"Lona," I said. "You know how you want to be a model?"

She nodded and ran her fingers through my hair.

"Well, I had a dream. It was a little freaky, but I want to tell it to you. Grandma said if you have a nightmare, you know, see something horrible about a person, you should tell as many people as you can so it won't come true."

I could feel her pull away, but I held her. "What did you see?"

"Lona," I said. "Give me a stack of Bibles cuz what I saw was your future."

She sat up. I couldn't stop now. "I saw that you and Dean were still together. You were older, maybe eight years from now."

"And—"

"And you've only gotten more beautiful, but the thing is—"

"What?"

"The thing is I saw you getting up to say good-bye to him as he went to work and he looked at you with hate in his eyes and said, 'You got uglier today.'"

Lona made a sound in her throat.

"And you believed it."

She looked around for her jacket. "I'm going now."

"No, wait. And the thing is, I could see something else, too. I saw your arms."

Lona stopped buttoning up her shirt. "What was wrong with them?"

"He gave you shitty tattoos so you couldn't model in anything other than long-sleeved shirts. It's like he'd stained you, and he—"

"He what?"

"He also knocked out half of your teeth on your right side, so you could never model close-ups, and your back—" I stopped. "He—"

She started to cry. "Kevin, I'm going now. You're scaring me."

I rose with her. "But you can change this. It doesn't have to happen. I've told you: Tell everyone. I'll do the same so it won't come true."

"You mean if I leave him and be with you, it'll be okay."

"No. It's not that. I'm telling you the truth. And your back," I tried, "he—"

"Kevin, don't ever speak to me again."

She left without tying her shoes or pulling on her jacket. At least she took the tape. She left, and nothing I could say would stop her from leaving.

It was true, Lona. My cousin's gonna take his time killing you. For years. And he'll do it from the inside out. I never told you I could see your tummy. He'd mauled your stomach with huge bite marks, and I won't tell you what I saw on your back—but we can stop it—or I can— in a few minutes.

I never told you I know a secret about you, Lona. It was one Grandma told me. It was around the exact second I fell in love with you.

Grandma told me that she took you and Dean out to Trapper's Point. She had the feeling. Her palms were burning. Gran showed you both what bear root looks like and asked you to find some while she pretended to pick cranberries. Dean went into the clearing first and came back empty-handed. You went in and returned with an armful.

"Bear root is what the bears love," Melanie, my grandma—my Eh Tsi—said. "It's medicine for the heart. It can clear arteries and make the heart muscles strong, and it only shows itself to a precious few."

So the root blossomed because it knew you were coming near.

You have medicine too, Lona, and that's why you've got to get away from Dean.

Cable TV's phone's ringing steady now that I'm broadcasting the footage from the game. The callers were people laughing hard and thanking me for a great job. I sprinkle an eighth of a gram on tobacco and roll it up. Voilà, Cocoa Puff! I love how coke makes a joint sweet. As always, my lips, tongue, and gums go numb as a smoke that smells like vanilla surrounds me.

"You're gonna make a great teacher!" Mrs. Spencer said. "They say the worst students make the best teachers, and I believe it!"

What a sheep. Mrs. Spencer taught me kindergarten ages ago, and she's still teaching it today.

"Thanks," I said. "How's your daughter?"

"Twins!" she chimed. "I'm a grandma!"

"Glad to hear it!" I hung up. Good thing I banged her before she got knocked up. I picked up the other line.

"Hey, Kev! It's Shari. You really were serious about being a teacher, weren't you! You'll do it! You'll do it!"

The hell with Black Fonzy! I was flying. "Thanks, Skull Face! Thanks a lot!" I yelled before hanging up. I took a puff, a swig, a sip, a shot. I popped two little Ephy's just to keep things fine. Back on top, baby.

I figured the town knew what a good job I'd done, so I took the phone off the hook. There will be no distractions for what is about to unfold. I lit a smoke. Maybe tobacco is the devil's hair. Did anyone ever think of that? Does anyone in this town know that the Chinese called TB "the Steaming Bone Disease?" Who knows? Who cares? Tomorrow I will be requesting a number of reference letters from key individuals, including Mr. Chang, plus working on a five-hundred-word essay called "Why I Want to Be a Teacher." This I can write in my sleep, as it seems my focus has never been clearer. Let the sheep talk amongst themselves. I am going to be a teacher!

"No more Hash Wednesdays!" I jigged. "No more Spring Bakes!" I danced a Spruce King dance, stopping to slap my ass and go, "Hoot hoot!"

I did the last of my coke and looked out the window. Hey! Still snowing and I'm glowing! Thank God it's snowing in Fort Simmer! Grandma always called snow the quietest mass.

Now for the real reason I agreed to tape the hockey game.

The moment of truth.

After Sandy finishes telling the western Northwest Territories what a great tutor I was, I turned the camera around to me and said, "Hello, party people. This is Kevin Garner. Yes, I know, the contraband kid. I just wanted to take this opportunity to say hi to Lona and my cousin Dean. Dean Meddows, if you don't know, is my cousin. I love him. I really do. The only problem is I'm in love with Lona Saw. Yup, that's right. I'm declaring this here and now." I stop to wipe my nose with my sleeve. "You see, folks, a few nights ago I had this dream where I saw Lona and Dean together, and they were miserable." I wait. "I had this dream Dean was beating on her on a daily basis and he was taking his time killing her, and I had a dream that she was brainwashed into thinking she needed to stay. Well, Lona Saw. You don't have to stay. You can leave. I don't want you to be beaten. I want you to be a model. Put Fort Simmer on the map. Make us proud. Lord knows, I'm trying. So that's it. Tell everyone about this. Tell everyone that Kevin Garner had a dream in which he saw the future of Dean Meddows and Lona Saw, and it was horrible. It was an early death for all of them, and even me, too. So that's it, folks. That's all. I'd like to dedicate tonight's game in memory of my grandma: Melanie Snow. Thank you and *mahsi cho*."

I turned the camera around and got back to the game.

I turn off the monitor and sound and the hockey game resumes, televised and broadcasting.

It's done. History's being rewritten via the moccasin

telegraph as each townie tells two friends and those two friends tell their two friends. You're free, Lona. If you stay, well, it's your fault now. I tried. When Dean starts in on you, you'll remember me. Besides—and I don't even mean this—I got Aleaha waiting for me in room 304.

As for your back, well, this is what I saw: Dean had you convinced you needed to learn about "reaction time." Every afternoon, you'd sit on the bed and he'd sit behind you. He'd hold a fresh cigarette behind you as you stared at the wall. The game was, the closer you felt the heat, the quicker you were supposed to move. Would it be today? Tomorrow? Friday? Next week? You never really caught on, Lona, that it was whenever he felt like it, and you were too slow and too beat to move away.

Now Lona. How in the hell could I think of something that cruel all by myself if I didn't see it?

I stood and made a toast: "One for the road and two for the ditch. Either way, I just rewrote history. Get out of this town, Lona, but take me with you. "

I crank WASP on the ghetto blaster. Blacky Lawless is blaring, "I WANNA BE SOMEBODY! BE SOMEBODY NOW!"

What the—I look out the window: pitch-black, snowing. Man, it's really coming down!

Grandma said when it snows, nothing can touch you. No bad medicine. Nothing. Look at the flakes! As thick as tufts of goose down. Oh, Lona, baby. I am so completely yours. My truck. We'd cruise, shack up, make love all night. We could watch the snow fall together for the rest

63

of our lives. I've never made love all night with someone. I've never wanted to hold someone so close to me and to whisper their name with love. To feel your hair, to move inside you. Such a beautiful face. I want to feel my skin under your nails. You blew it, baby. You're going out with the wrong cousin. With your atrocious perfume and your beautiful brown Metis eyes.

Look at that snow. Grandma said if you catch the last of the winter's snowfall, that snow is called the Snow of the Virgin Mary because Mary called it for the world. If you melt this snow and bottle it and drink it or rub it on a wound or a burn, it can cure anything. Maybe this is it. Maybe this is Grandma telling me everything'll be okay.

What am I gonna do about Leo? Leo took me in after Grandma passed, gave me the lowdown in the prettiest house in Simmer. We sat down, had some tea. Joey was there in his flashy suit. I had always seen these guys around town when I was growing up. They were so cool. We listened to some Neil Young, passed a thick fatty around, and sipped African tea.

"Sorry about your grandmother," Leo said. "Anything you need?"

"A job would be nice."

"Check this out." Leo broke down the science of dealing to me and finished with a simple question. "You in?"

The language they used, the codes, the poetry of it all. I never felt so alive in my whole life. I nodded. "I'm in."

Leo smiled. "This is your Freedom Thirty-five plan, Kevin. I'm going to start you moving quarters. That all right? Joey here will teach you how to use the scales and eye it up. Remember: Although the customer is never right, never underestimate one. Most frequent flyers have scales at home and will hunt you down if you screw 'em, so don't. Do it right. Take pride in your work and watch your ass." He and Joey pointed in unison to a sign on the wall that read "Watch Thy Ass!" before continuing: "If a customer has a great experience with a company, they'll tell four to six people. If they're screwed over by a company, they'll tell fourteen to twenty people. Prevention is the key. You keep 'em satisfied, they'll always come back. You got that?"

I never felt so good in my whole life. "I got it, Leo. Thank you for this."

Leo stood up. "We take care of our own. Dogribs are outnumbered in Fort Simmer, and I had great respect for your grandmother. She and my mom were like sisters. We'll work together, right? It's about getting paid."

"And laid," Joey said. "Welcome to the club."

Leo shook my hand like a man. Joey, too. That week I made three grand cash. Cash. You're damn right I felt great. I got my truck within three months, and this trailer is already all mine.

Whoah. Two Summits blast by the building, kicking up mud and snow. Soon, half this town will be flying through the fields and ditches on their Ski-Doos for a last grab at winter glory. Hoo-yah.

There's kids making snowmen. One shakes a tree, dousing himself with snow. The headlights of a car pull

65

into the driveway. The white palm of the light when it turns the corner catches the houses across the street, grabs each house, and pushes it down. The car door opens. Someone sprints toward the building. Pizza boy: probably Jesse Chaplin, the Chief's son. Third-biggest dealer in town. Now that I'm gonna be in TEP, now that I've set Aleaha free, he can keep the tip. I pull out my twenty and open the door. All I hear is yelling: "Three little pygmies! Three little pygmies! Disconnect! Disconnect!"

"What?" I ask. I don't understand. The music's too loud. It's not Jesse. It's Mr. Chang! He slaps me hard across the face, "Turn it off! Turn it off! Turn off the computer! Stop the tape! Stop the tape!"

I'm stunned. He flies to the monitor and turns it on. I can't believe what I see. My heart twists and my stomach sucks it down. Through the smoke. On the monitor. On the broadcast that Fort Smith, Hay River, Fort Simpson, and Yellowknife are watching, a naked Nurse Nora is chasing three studs with piggy masks on. The men squeal like pigs, and I've never realized until now what a cheap set they've used. A porno!

Three Little Piggies.

My ears are ringing louder than they were this morning. The communities are seeing a porno. My porno. How? I can't believe it. I've been playing a porno! My porno. For how long? The nasty-ass porno I thought I lost forever. How the—?

Nurse Nora bellows, "I'll huff and I'll puff and I'll blowwwwww your house down!"

WASP is still blaring, "I WANNA BE SOMEBODY! BE SOMEBODY NOW!"

I have watched this porno a hundred times at the Love Shack. Ron Jeremy is still skinny in this one. He cracks a few good jokes before going to town. "I WANNA BE SOMEBODY! BE SOME—" Mr. Chang bangs the ghetto blaster off, rips at the cables, pulls them right out of the console. He's swearing in Chinese at me. At me! His hood slides off his head. He looks at me. His face is red. "Ho Cha! Hockey game ended after you made your little speech! I've been calling here, but you didn't answer!"

My mind is a whirlwind of rate-limiting steps that begin to eat themselves as they swirl and die together. Did I turn the Record button off by accident?

My right cheek burns.

"Get out!" he yells. Spit lands on his wolverine hood. He's waiting for me to respond. I look to the little red hand of his that slapped me and then to his purple, puckered lips.

"I WANNA BE SOMEBODY! BE SOMEBODY NOW!"

Sandy. God. He watched the broadcast, saw it all. Mr. Chang ejects the tape and grabs the twenty from my palm, holding it in front of his face. "Out!" he says. "Get out! I'm gonna lose my license, you sonovabitch!"

My head falls back. The label on the porno he ejected was switched with a blank label. This was the one. I was supposed to tape "WWF Raw" over this one on Saturday.

I feel the cold winter air bathe me from the open door behind, and I use up fifteen minutes of air in the next two seconds. Tomorrow, Black Fonzy—the Fist of God—is gonna be looking for me for calling his old lady Skull Face. Tomorrow the community'll be talking about me at the coffee shop. Everyone's gonna know my name. Everyone! I'm dead. I'm so dead. I feel my rib cage rise and fall as I release a death sigh to the ceiling.

Grandma, you lied. Anything and anyone can touch you in the snow. . . .

Who wants me now? I got an ounce on the street and one in my pack. My name is Kevin Garner. I wanted to be a teacher. I turn and I go, dizzy through the snow as it pops and crunches under my feet. To the women's residence. Aleaha. Leo. Constable Morris. Bury me deep, somebody, under this snow of deceit. . . .

Sandy . . .

Lona . . .

Anyone . . .

Crow

LINDA HOGAN

Even though she always has peppermint in her apron pockets, nobody much visits Grandma anymore. Once in a while my brother, Buster, stops by to pick me up and we go out to the flats to see her. Or someone who has moved away returns to town on their summer vacation to look over their old home place, trying to pick up the lost pieces of their lives, wanting stories about their kin. They stop by to ask my grandmother where old so-and-so has gone. More often than not, she directs them to the cemetery, peppermint candy in their hands.

"That bag goes out to the car." I point at the brown paper sack. Buster moves the coleus plants and the clay sheep that has grass sprouting from its back like green wool. He snoops in the bag. "The cookies are in the cupboard," I tell him.

He opens the cupboard and rummages around for the

Oreos. I have just enamelled the kitchen and the cabinet doors stick. "Leave them open," I say to Buster. I inspect the kitchen before leaving for Grandma's. It passes my scrutiny, the clean blue paint and the new tablecloth I made of white strawberry-print cotton.

We pack up Buster's Chevy with my clothes, the groceries, my dog, Teddy, and the radio I bought for Grandma. We drive past the Drunkard Brethren Church. There are some people, perhaps the choir, standing outside in dark robes. I think we look pretty flashy, passing by in the gold Chevrolet with shining chrome, and the bumper stickers saying "Indian Affairs Are the Best" and "Pilgrim, Go Home." I sit very straight with my eyelids lowered, even though inside my body I am exhilarated, enjoying this ride in my brother's car. We drive past the stand of scrub oak and then turn off the paved road into the silence that exists between towns. The crows fly up off the road, cursing at us. Since his wife isn't along, Buster accelerates and lets the car go almost as fast as it will, "tying on the tachs." We speed along. "I clocked her at one ten," he says. He slows down by the cornfields and paces himself on out through the flatlands where Grandma lives. It has been raining and everything is moist and bright, the outlines of the buildings cleaner than usual.

When we pull off the road at Grandma's, I stay in the car a few minutes to look at the morning glories she has planted. They are blooming, the blue flowers on a vined arch over the old front door. The heaven-blue circles nod in the ozone-smelling breeze.

Teddy is anxious to get out and go searching for moles. He whines and paces across the backseat. "Let that damn dog out," Buster says, but he opens the door before I can turn around and get to it. Teddy runs out barking, his tail pulling him sideways with joy. Grandma hears. She comes to the door and stands waiting in the shade, surrounded by the morning glories on her front steps. She already has her hand in her apron pocket, ready to lure us with peppermint, when Teddy turns and circles back viciously, barking at a car that has pulled up silently behind us. I didn't hear the limousine drive up, and now Teddy is all around it, barking and raging at the waxed, shining dark metal of the car, and at its tires that remain miraculously clean, even driving through the mud.

"Theodore!" I yell out his proper name, reserved for reprimands and orders. Teddy continues to bark, his golden tail down between his short dingo legs, his claws digging into the wet red clay. The chauffeur ignores him and goes around stiffly to open the back car door.

Grandma is taking it all in, looking proud and pompous. She respects money, but she hates those people who have it. All money is dirty, she has said. It all started with the Rockefellers and their ilk. Now she remains standing very straight and tall, her hand still in the blue-flowered pocket, while a woman is let out of the car and begins walking across the chicken yard. The white woman's shoes are expensive. They are rich beige leather, and I feel tense watching her heels dig into the clay soil and the chicken droppings. The muddy clay tries to suck the woman down. The chickens make a path for her, scurrying off and clucking. A copper hen that has been roosting in a tree falls out and screeches, runs off muddy, waddling.

I recognize the lady. She stopped in once for a meal at the Hamburger Heaven where Buster used to work. She was out of place, and the customers and employees all stared at her. She made them uneasy and they alternately talked too much and too loud, or they were silent. When the order was ready, Buster took several plates around the room and stopped at the woman's table, flustered. He was overly serious in his discomfort, his face tense. Like an accusation, he said, "You're the hamburger." Laughter floated up into the entire room.

I step out close to hear the conversation between Grandma and the woman. Grandma's jaw is tight like trouble is in the air. While they talk, I pull a stamen from a morning glory and suck it.

"I'd like to buy two dozen eggs," says the beige shoe lady, opening her pocketbook and releasing the odor of French perfume and money.

"We're all out of eggs." Grandma still has her hand in her pocket. She avoids looking at the woman's face. She looks past her at the horizon. It is the way she looks through city people, or people with money, as though they aren't there.

"I'll take a bag of feed then." The woman is thin and wispy. Her hair falls forward as she opens her wallet. The bills are neatly ordered. I can't help but notice Grandma's eyes on them.

"Haven't had any feed delivered from the co-op as late," says Grandma nonchalantly. Grandma is the local distributor of feed grain and Watkins products, including the cherry-flavored drink mix. She keeps an entire room neatly stocked with bags of grains and bottles of vanilla, aspirin, vitamins, and liniment. And she sells eggs. It is how she supports all those chickens, she claims.

Grandma offers the woman a mint, but the woman refuses and grows huffy. "Probably the diet type," I hear Buster say under his breath, and I'm sure the woman overheard him because she is clearly put out, and says to Grandma, "Why don't you close all the way down or put a sign out?"

"I'm fixing to once you leave." I can feel a smile under Grandma's words even though her face has no expression and her eyes are blank, staring off into Kansas or some other distant state. The woman doesn't know she is being made fun of, and she wants something else, I can tell. She wants to help Grandma out, to be good to the less fortunate or something. It is often that way with the rich. But it seems to me that there are some barriers in life that can't be passed through by good deeds or money. Like the time I found a five-dollar bill on the floor of the movie theater and felt like a thief for picking it up. It was a fire in my pocket. On the way home I saw a man going through the trash, collecting cans to cash in. I took out the bill and handed it to him. I said I just found it and maybe it was his. He took it, but there was a dreadful and shameful look on his face, and I knew then that everyone ought to stay in their own place, wherever that may be, without trespassing on other people's lives. Maybe money just goes where it wants and leaves the rest of us alone.

But Grandma will not be shamed, even though the house looks dilapidated in contrast to the woman and her car. Grandma is proud enough still to plant the flowers and water them with the blue plastic pitcher.

The woman returns to the limousine and they drive away. If it weren't for the recent rain, the car would have covered the morning glories in a cloud of dust. I wonder what it is that made the chauffeur so anxious to leave.

"Last week she wanted to buy the house," Grandma says, and takes out two lint-covered peppermint kisses and gives one each to me and Buster.

"This old place?" Buster has no tact. I give him one of my looks which he has said could kill, but he goes on talking. "How much did she offer you? You should have taken it." His cheek is swollen with peppermint. "You are probably sitting on an oil well."

But Grandma loves her home and will never leave it as long as she lives.

Now and then she is in a bad mood, and this is going to be one of those times. Her eyes are sullen. I remind myself of her better moments. Out loud I say to Buster, "Remember the day we took Grandma to town? When she was in such a good humor that she went up to that tall policeman and asked, 'Do you know where any trouble is?'"

Buster's smile begins on the left side of his face, but

Grandma ignores what I say. She hands me the egg basket. "Sis, why don't you go out and gather up the eggs?"

Teddy is overjoyed to go with me, looking in the corners of the barn, the storage shed, under old tires on the ground. I find a few eggs in new places, in a batch of damp grass, under the morning glories. Teddy runs in circles, and the crows fly up around us. They remind me of stories, like how Old Crow Raven used to be white, white snowy feathers, marble white beak and claws, until one day he got too sure of himself and offered to go to an island of fire and bring back a coal for the two-legged, unwinged people. As he descended to the island, following the orange flames and black smoke billowing up from a hollow tree, he was overcome with the heat and blinded by a thick dark cloud of smoke. Disoriented, he flew straight into the flames and was scorched. That is the reason, people say, why the crows are black. Grandma's theory is that the bird went for the wrong reasons. He didn't really care about the people at all. He just wanted to prove his worth.

When I go inside and set the eggs on the table, Grandma is on one of her lectures about how people are just like blackbirds except they are paling. "Money is turning everybody to white," she says. "All the Indians are going white. Oh, I suppose they still care about their little ones and go to church on Sunday, but all they've got their minds on is the almighty dollar." She stops abruptly while I recount the eggs. There are thirty-one of them, and what with yesterday's eggs around the house, she could have sold the woman four dozen or so. She fixes her gaze on me, and the whites around her dark pupils startle me. Even the eggs seem to wobble on the unlevel table. "How come you never come to visit me anymore? I have a hundred grandchildren and no one ever comes out here." It's no use arguing, so I don't answer.

"They're all trying to make a buck, Grandma," Buster says.

Most of the time Grandma doesn't have anyone to talk to and she gets lonely. All of my cousins have been breaking away like spiders, going to cities, to California, marrying and moving. That's why I brought her the radio.

"I don't want to hear anything about money or bucks." Her jaw is tight. She looks straight at Buster.

I turn on the water in the sink and the sound of it running drowns out Grandma's voice. She is still talking about all the Indians out here acting like white people, and about how no one comes to see her. "Those men bullying their sons," she says. "They shoot the birds right out of the air. And money, I wouldn't touch that stuff if you paid me to." And then she notices the radio and becomes quiet. "What's this?"

I dry my hands and plug it in. "I brought it for you. I thought you might like some music." I turn the station selector.

Buster says, "You can talk to *that* thing all you want."

I put it on a gospel station, because that is her favorite music. But it's only a man talking and he has a bad voice. "I know my mother went to heaven, harumph, and I had

76

a brother who died and I know he went to heaven." The man clears his throat. "One by one, we uh, proceed, our candles lighted. We, you, you, I, I think that maybe some of those Europeans haven't reached the heights of Christianity, harumph, that we have, but maybe we have really gone below them and maybe we have, uh, wronged them."

Buster imitates a rooster, his fists in his armpits. "Bock bock," he says. I give him a dirty look.

"Don't you make fun," Grandma says. "The first time I ever heard a radio, don't you know, was Coolidge's inaugural address."

And she starts in again, right over the voice of the radio, about how no one comes to talk to her and how we don't even call her on the telephone. Buster gets angry. He says she's getting senile, and he walks out the door and slams it. Grandma and I are silent because he walked out stiff and angry, and the radio says, "I got saved from the sermons you preach, uh, that's what he said, and from the sermons on your pages in the mail."

I'm still thinking about going to heaven with a candle, but I hear Buster outside, scurrying around. I look out the window but can't tell what he's doing.

When he returns, he is carrying a crow and tracking in red mud. "How did you catch that?" I ask. Its eyes are wild, but it is beautiful with black feathers shining like silk and velvet. I go closer to look at it. "Can I touch it?" I put my hand over the bird. "Is it hurt?"

Buster pulls back and looks me in the eye. His look

scares me. He is too intense, and his eyes are darker than usual. He takes hold of the wing. "Don't," I say, but he grabs that glorious coal-colored wing and twists it.

"Buster!" I yell at him and the crow cries out too.

He throws it down on the floor. I'm too afraid to move. "Now don't say no one comes to see you. That damn crow won't leave. You can tell him all you want how nobody comes to see you." Buster stalks out, and we hear the car engine start. I am standing, still unable to move, looking at the bird turning circles on the floor, and beginning to cry. "Oh, Grandma, how could Buster be so awful?" I go down to pick up the injured bird, but it tries to get away. I don't blame it. There's no reason to be trusting. Grandma is sad too, but she just sits at the table, and I know we are both thinking of Buster's cruelty and we are women together for the first time.

I turn off the radio, and I am thinking of all the poor earthly creatures.

There is a cardboard box in the Watkins room, so I go in to get it for the bird and notice that the room is full of the feed Grandma refused to sell the beige shoe lady.

Grandma has already broken a stick and is fitting it to the bird's wing. It is quiet in her hands. I strip off a piece of red calico cotton from her quilting cloth. She takes it in her wrinkled hand and wraps the smooth wing.

"I hate him," I say. "He's always been mean." But Grandma doesn't say anything. She is busy with the crow and has placed it in the box on a nest of paper towels.

"I guess that's what happens to people who think

about money all the time," she says. "They forget about the rest of life. They pay no mind to the hurts of each other or the animals. But the Bible teaches me not to judge them." Still, she says nothing else about money or visitors.

The crow listens when Grandma talks. For several days it has been nodding its head at her and following her with its eyes. It listens to the gospel radio, too. "That crow is a heartbreaker," she says. "Just look at him." I hope it isn't true. It is a lovely bird, and sometimes it cries out weakly. It has warm black wings and eyes made of stolen corn. I am not a crow reverencer, but I swear that one night I heard it talking to Grandma and it was saying that no one comes to visit.

Grandma is telling it a story about the crows. "They were people and used to speak our tongues," she tells it. It listens. It is raining outside and the rain is hitting the windows. The earth is full of red puddles, and they are moving. Somewhere outside, a door is slamming open and closed in the wind.

"You'd like that rainwater," she tells the crow. "Make your feathers soft."

Though I am mad at Buster, I can see that he was right. This bird and Grandma are becoming friends. She feeds it grain and corn. It rides on her shoulder and is the color her hair used to be. Crow pulls at the strands of her gray hair. It is like Grandma has shed a skin. She is new and soft, a candlelight inside her.

"Bird bones heal pretty fast," she tells me. "Not like ours."

"Can we listen to something besides gospel for a while?" I ask her. She ignores the question, so I go into the bedroom to read a magazine and take a nap. The phone rings and I hear Grandma talking and then the radio goes off and the front door opens and closes. I get up and go out into the kitchen, but it is silent, except for the bird picking at the cardboard box.

For a moment I consider putting him out in the rain, splint and all, he looks so forlorn. But Grandma would never forgive me. I ask him, "Have you heard that money is evil?"

Teddy is barking at the front door. It's Buster. Even the dog is unkind to him, growling back in his throat. Buster wants to see if we need anything or if I am ready to go home. I don't speak to him, and he sits down on the sofa to read the paper. I stay in the kitchen with Crow.

A house without its tenant is a strange place. I notice for the first time that without Grandma's presence, the house smells of Vicks and old wool. Her things look strange and messy; even the doilies on the couch and end tables are soiled. The walls are sweating and the plaster is stained. I can see Buster sitting on the sofa reading the paper and I decide to tell him I think he is beyond forgiveness.

"Leave me alone." He stands up. His pants ride low and he puts his hands in his pockets and pushes the pants down lower. It is a gesture of intimidation. "She's got company, hasn't she? And maybe that crow will teach her how to behave." He says he is bringing a cage, and I say a cage is no place for a wild bird that longs to be outside in the free air. We are about to get into it when Grandma returns. She is crying.

"I ought to kill myself," she says.

We grow quiet and we both look down at the floor. I have never seen her cry except at funerals, and I sneak glances up at her now and then while she is crying, until she tells me, "Quit gawking. I just lost all my money."

"Your money?" I am struck stupid. I am surprised. I know she never believed in banks, and I thought she didn't believe much in money, either. I didn't know she had any. I worry about how much she lost. By her tears, I can tell it wasn't just the egg money.

"I hid it in the umbrella because I was scared of robbers, and I lost it in the rain. When I went back looking for it, it wasn't there." She checks inside the wet umbrella, opening and closing it as if she couldn't believe in the money's absence, running her hand around the spokes. "I forgot I hid it there. I just plain forgot," she wails. "I used to keep it in the cupboard until I heard about the burglars."

There is a circle of water around her on the floor and her face is broken, but she takes two pieces of peppermint from her pocket and absently hands one to each of us, the old habit overpowering grief. "I think I should have sold that woman the eggs."

She has a lot of sorrow bending her back. "I walked up

the road as fast as I could, but it was already gone."

She becomes as quiet as the air between towns. I turn on the radio, and it sounds like a funeral with "We Shall Gather at the River." Grandma picks up Crow, and he seems to leap right to her chest and balance there on one of the old ivory buttons. She reaches into her left pocket and takes out grains of corn.

Grandma's shoes are ruined. She puts them on the stove to dry, but they are already curling upward at the toes and the leather soles are coming apart.

"How's your kids, Buster?"

"Pretty good," he says, but he looks glum. He's probably worried about his lost inheritance.

"How's Flora?"

Buster has his ready-made answers. "Well," he drawls, "by the time I met her I knew what happiness was."

I chime in, mocking, "But it was too late to do anything about it." I finish the sentence with him. Grandma looks at me, startled, and is silent a moment, and then she begins to laugh.

There's nothing else to do, so I get up. "Grandma, you want some eggs?" I turn on the stove. "I'll cook up some eggs and cornmeal pancakes." I wonder how much money she had hidden away.

"I'm all out of molasses," she says. "Plumb out."

"Buster will go to the store and get some. Won't you, Buster?"

"In this rain?" But he looks at me, and I look stern. "Oh, sure, yeah, I'll be right back." And he carefully folds the paper and picks up his keys and goes to the door. He is swallowed up by the blowing torrents of water.

I take Grandma's shoes off the stove and put them by the back door.

"Edna fell down the stairs last night," Grandma says, an explanation of where she has been. "Broke her hip."

"How is she?"

"I didn't get to see her. Because of the money. Maybe Buster will take me."

I put some batter in the pan and it sizzles. Crow chatters back at it and it sounds like he is saying how hard it is to be old. I want to put my hand on Grandma's shoulder, but I don't. Instead I go to the window and look out. Crow's lovers or cousins are bathing in the puddles of rainwater, washing under their wings and shaking their feathers. I think Crow is the one who went to that island after fire and now, even though his body is so much like the night sky, he is doomed to live another life. I figure he's going to stay here with Grandma to make up for his past mistakes. I think Grandma is right about almost everything. I feel lonely. I go over and touch her. She clasps my hand tightly and then lets go and pats it. "Your pancakes are burning," she says.

Ice

JOSEPH BRUCHAC

In memory of Swift Eagle

An eagle. It whistles once, a voice that pierces the dawn as it opens its wings. Then it spreads those great dark wings wider, jumps from the top of the scarred old hemlock into the cold sky. Its wings cup the air and it flaps up, glides, flaps again with an ease unrivaled by any human-made flying machine. It locks its wings as it finds a thermal and soars, eyes sharper than those of any other being of land or sky, scanning the widening earth beneath it for signs of life. Its flight carries it over the top of Brown Mountain, above the bare ledges where the rattlesnakes basked two seasons ago, their bodies laid out on the ancient bedrock like lazy lightning. Now, as a thin skin of ice covers the flat stones, the rattlesnakes lie denned, wrapped together in a survival knot far under the surface.

As it soars, the eagle watches the surface of the lake, seeking the silver flash of a feeding trout. Though still high above, its dive can bring it down, claws outspread, in a matter of heartbeats. But the old lake between the mountains, although unfrozen, is quiet today. Something, though, keeps drawing that eagle on, over the islands in the narrows, past camps and motels closed for the winter, boats hauled up for winter storage, the black undulating strip of road near the water as quiet as a sleeping snake. There is a song that reaches the eagle—not just its ears, but in a deeper place.

And there, at last, at the lower end of the lake, the eagle sees something on the water. The one boat that is out this cold morning. Not a birchbark canoe, though it might as well be. The old man who sits in the front of the rowboat is chanting old and familiar words in a language deeper in this land than the roots of any of the oldest trees. True, he wears the kind of ceremonial headdress that was never seen in this neck of the woods two hundred years ago, its black and white feathers taken from the tail of another eagle that once soared over the plains far toward the sunset. But that is what people expect nowadays, especially the anxious town fathers of Lake George who watch from the pier near the Million Dollar Beach, not far from where the paddlewheel tourist boat, the *Minnehaha*, departs for summer cruises.

I've worked on that boat two summers now, selling hot dogs and nachos from the snack bar, and it is not that bad a gig for a high school kid like me. No need for beads and feathers, most folks not giving even a passing thought to my slightly darker complexion. Probably, if they notice at all, they assume I'm Italian or maybe Puerto Rican. Not a homegrown immigrant in his own land. One who, though proud of his heritage, sees nothing wrong with keeping a low profile every now and then, even if the damn boat's name does make you want to gag. Plus, having aspirations of becoming a writer myself, it gives me an opportunity to study the customs of those strange beings called flatlanders. Kind of like Vladimir Nabokov, that lecherous old Russian novelist. You know, the guy who wrote *Lolita*.

Uncle Tommy, who was working buildings and grounds at Cornell in the 1950s, said the old bird used to ride the buses in Ithaca, New York, with a notebook, sitting behind junior high school girls on their way home and writing down every word they said.

Uncle Tommy shook his head when he told me that. But it wasn't that Uncle Tommy was disapproving of old Vlad stalking those giggly prepubescents. It was more personal.

"I talked to him too," Uncle Tommy said. "Plenty of times. Yeah, he knew me. It got to the point where when he would see me over raking by Goldwyn Smith Hall he would make it a point to come up and say 'So, Chief, vot vill the veather be, zis fine day?' But did he write down anything I told him? In all that stuff he wrote about America, is there even one word about a real Indian?"

The old Indian man in the front of that rowboat reaches into his pouch and casts something onto the water. He calls out loud words in a language that none of the town fathers on the shore can understand, but it makes them nod their heads in approval. They are getting their money's worth. There are two film crews from the Albany TV stations, come seventy miles to see this and devote at least twenty seconds of sarcastic commentary to it on the eleven o'clock news. I have no doubt they approve of the way the wise elder stands up in the boat's bow and spreads his arms dramatically wide, though they don't hear him mutter, "Oh, shit!" under his breath when he loses his balance for just a second and almost pitches into the icy waters before he regains his equilibrium.

Lake George is spring fed, one of the coldest lakes in the Adirondacks, and the fact that it hasn't frozen yet, even though it has been a warm winter so far with just about no snow, is kind of a mystery. No ice at all, and only a week until the annual Winter Carnival, a huge draw with its ice-fishing derby and snow sculptures, ice princesses, and outhouse races where gleeful crews of bartenders from the various lakeside bars and restaurants push fully-manned (waitressed, actually) two-holers on a hundred-yard course that is at present but a freeway for pike.

Chief Thomas Fox, wise and sagacious as Chingachook, is their last hope.

"Uncle Tommy, can we please go home now?" asks the last of the Mohegans, who is freezing his nuts off in the seat behind him.

"Just row, my nephew, just keep rowing," says my noble uncle.

So I try to flex my fingers, which I can no longer feel, grasp the oars more tightly, and start rowing. I shouldn't complain. It was my idea to be here with him.

In a purely genetic sense, Uncle Tommy isn't really my uncle. His second wife, Aunt Ruby, who took the star road five years ago, was my grandmother's sister. Uncle Tommy is Swenoga, which is a whole different tribe from Abenaki. But in the thirty years he has lived here in the mountains, he has listened and learned enough so that whenever I have questions about our Abenaki history and stories, it is Uncle Tommy I turn to. I even suffered through seven summers at Frontier Town with him, helping him run the archery concession in the Indian Village below Fort Custer. I was too young then to have read Dante's *Inferno*, but I currently recognize the setting of that tourist attraction as the Seventh Circle of Hell for Indians. Reading above my grade level has been my specialty since hitting sixth grade in Long Lake School, and I haven't slowed down since.

Anyhow, our little aboriginal tipis were next to the bear cages. I don't know who had more peanuts and dumb comments thrown at them by kids (and, yup, their parents), us or our furry relatives.

That was a bonding experience for all of us—Uncle Tommy, me, and the bears. I used to talk to them and scratch them behind their ears when nobody was looking. Except for Uncle Tommy. He would sit and talk with them in his way. Not with words, but with silence and maybe a song or two. When he drove me home at night in his Ford pickup truck, Uncle Tommy would talk about the bears more often than the people.

"They told me today they are lonely for the mountains and the rivers," he said one night as he rounded the turn to Long Lake.

"But weren't they raised in captivity?" I asked.

"That's why they been asking me about the mountains and the rivers."

When the tourist business died off to the point that the owners decided to close the place down, no one was quite sure what they were going to do with those bears. There was general agreement that you couldn't just let a bear go in the woods. "Humane injection," a term I truly love, was finally decided upon. Good morning, Dr. Death. Except when the day came to put the bears down, those four fat bruins were gone. Three days later Uncle Tommy came back from his vacation in Canada. I helped him take the cap off his pickup and clean it out.

When I heard Lake George was hiring Uncle Tommy to try to bring the ice, I called him up. I planned to ask him if he needed my help. He is way over seventy years old now, even if he doesn't look it. By that I mean he looks as if he is at least a hundred. He had three sons by his first marriage, back when he was riding the rodeo circuit— which put an end to his first marriage. But all three of them were killed in battle, one in Vietnam, one in Grenada, and one, who rodeoed like Uncle Tommy, in a bar in Tulsa. Uncle Tommy does have some grandkids out in Oklahoma, but their mom has kept them out of touch with Uncle Tommy since it was her husband who lost his battle with the bottle. So it is kind of like I am the only young and strong relative available to help him when he needs it. Which is okay by me. He also reads everything I write and critiques it for me. He is pretty good at that. He still reads a lot, and when he was young he had some of his poems published in an anthology put out by the Bureau of Indian Affairs. So I was ready to volunteer. But I didn't have to.

"Nephew," he said as soon as he picked up the phone. "Can you be here in two hours?"

"Unh-hun," I said. Which was my entire side of the conversation with him.

"Bring that new story along, Mitchell," he said. "I'll read it while you drive."

I've been working on a series of stories. Sort of Indian time travel. The main character, who is a modern Indian with a good grasp of history, has invented a way to go back in time. He has discovered that all that separates the past from the present is something like a layer of ice. Most people walk on that ice. It is cloudy to some and clear to others, but the past is always there below them, locked away and out of reach. But this Indian scientist has found a way to break through the ice, to make a hole in it so he can dive through. What he does is to study history very carefully and then go back to the places where bad things happened to Indians. All he takes with him is a blackjack. He has it worked out so that when he appears he is standing right behind the one crucial person just before he spoke those words or took those actions that made bad things happen.

For example, in my current tale, his target is James McLaughlin, the Indian agent (and author of *My Friend, the Indian*) who gave the order to arrest Sitting Bull at Grand River, which led to Sitting Bull's being killed by a group of Indian policemen. My protagonist sets his coordinates carefully and appears right behind McLaughlin late Sunday afternoon of December 14, 1890. *Whomp!*

After I'd helped Uncle Tommy load his regalia into the back of my jeep, I handed him my story. It was only ten pages long. The last four pages explain how Buffalo Bill arrives at Grand River the day after Sitting Bull's original death, and talks his old friend into going with him on an eastern tour with his Wild West Show. A chance meeting in Chicago with Crazy Horse (saved in one of my earlier tales) leads to the two of them founding the American Indian Movement seven decades before Dennis Banks and Russell Means.

As always, Uncle Tommy read it twice and then didn't say anything for another ten miles. As always, he outwaited me.

"Well," I said.

"Good writing," he said. "As usual. Far as I know, you got the history right too. But I wonder about all this hitting people over the head and knocking them unconscious. A concussion, that's no small thing. It isn't really that easy to knock somebody out."

Then he was silent for another ten miles before he continued his thought. "The one man I ever saw really get knocked out was in the merchant marine with me. Got hit in the back of the head by the blunt side of a loading hook. Knocked him cold as a codfish. Didn't dent his head in none, but when he finally came to he wasn't ever the same again." Uncle Tommy tapped the dashboard with one finger. "Liked to say the word 'macaroni.' Said it a lot after he got knocked out. That was about all he said."

"It's science fiction," I said.

"Ah," Uncle Tommy said. He tapped the dashboard again, a beat now that I recognized as a 49er, one of those good-time powwow drum songs. "James McLaughlin, distinguished Indian agent at Standing Rock." He looked over at me.

"Macaroni," we both said.

After we got done laughing, Uncle Tommy sighed. "Nephew," he said, "I understand your stories. Sometimes, though, all we can do is just the best we can. If we do that, we can still touch the past. If we do that, things happen."

I rowed and kept rowing. Every now and then Uncle Tommy sang and put out more tobacco. Ah, yes. Something was definitely happening. I had now lost all feeling up to my elbows. I rubbed my chin against my coat collar. I heard the rasp of cold flesh against wool, but didn't feel a thing. I was turning into ice. I found myself looking at the back of Uncle Tommy's head. I opened my mouth. But I didn't speak.

Uncle Tommy did. "Listen," he said.

The people on the dock were yelling something. They sounded excited. But that wasn't what Uncle Tommy meant.

A whistle came from the sky above us. I looked up. That was when I saw the eagle for the first time. It was circling above us, close enough that it was only an arrow shot away. It cocked its head and whistled again.

"Look," Uncle Tommy said.

I looked at the ice that was forming behind us, following us as we rowed toward shore, a swirl of ice covering the lake like the wings of the eagle spreading over the ancient and listening sky.

Wild Geese
(1934)

LOUISE ERDRICH

Nector Kashpaw

On Friday mornings, I go down to the sloughs with my brother Eli and wait for the birds to land. We have built ourselves a little blind. Eli has second sense and an aim I cannot match, but he is shy and doesn't like to talk. In this way it is a good partnership. Because I got sent to school, I am the one who always walks into town and sells what we shoot. I get the price from the Sisters, who cook for the priests, and then I come home and split the money in half. Eli usually takes his bottle off into the woods, while I go into town, to the fiddle dance, and spark the girls.

So there is a Friday near sundown, the summer I am out of school, that finds me walking up the hill with two geese slung from either wrist, tied with leather bands. Just to set the record clear, I am a good-looking boy, tall and slim, without a belly hanging in the way. I can have the pick of girls, is what I'm saying. But that doesn't matter anyhow, because I have already decided that Lulu Nanapush is the one. She is the only one of them I want.

I am thinking of her while I walk—those damn eyes of hers, sharp as ice picks, and the curl of her lips. Her figure is round and plush, yet just at the edge of slim. She is small, yet she will never be an armful or an eyeful because I'll never get a bead on her. I know that even now. She never stops moving long enough for me to see her all in a piece. I catch the gleam on her hair, the flash of her arm, a sly turn of hip. Then she is gone. I think of her little wet tongue and I have to stop then and there, in my tracks, at the taste that floods into my mouth. She is a tart berry full of juice, and I know she is mine. I cannot wait for the night to start. She will be waiting in the bush.

Because I am standing there, lost on the empty road, half drowned in the charms of Lulu, I never see Marie Lazarre barrel down. In fact, I never even hear her until it is too late. She comes straight down like a wagon unbraked, like a damn train. Her eye is on me, glaring under a stained strip of sheet. Her hand is wound tight in a pillowcase like a boxer's fist.

"Whoa," I say, "slow down girl."

"Move aside," she says.

She tries to pass. Out of reflex I grab her arm, and then I see the initialed pillowcase. SHC is written on it in letters red as wine. Sacred Heart Convent. What is it doing on her arm? They say I am smart as a whip around here, but this time I am too smart for my own good. Marie

Lazarre is the youngest daughter of a family of horse-thieving drunks. Stealing sacred linen fits what I know of that blood, so I assume she is running off with the Sisters' pillowcase and other valuables. Who knows? I think a chalice might be hidden beneath her skirt. It occurs to me, next moment, I may get a money bonus if I bring her back.

And so, because I am saving for the French-style wedding band I intend to put on the finger of Lulu Nanapush, I do not let Marie Lazarre go down the hill.

Not that holding on to her is easy.

"Lemme go, you damn Indian," she hisses. Her teeth are strong looking, large and white. "You stink to hell!"

I have to laugh. She is just a skinny white girl from a family so low you cannot even think they are in the same class as Kashpaws. I shake her arm. The dead geese tied to my wrist swing against her hip. I never move her. She is planted solid as a tree. She begins to struggle to get loose, and I look up the hill. No one coming from that direction, or down the road, so I let her try. I am playing with her. Then she kicks me with her hard-sole shoe.

"Little girl," I growl, "don't play with fire!"

Maybe I shouldn't do this, but I twist her arm and screw it up tight. Then I am ashamed of myself because tears come, suddenly, from her eyes and hang bitter and gleaming from her lashes. So I let up for a moment. She moves away from me. But it is just to take aim. Her brown eyes glaze over like a wounded mink's, hurt but still fighting vicious. She launches herself forward and rams her knee in my stomach.

I lose my balance and pitch over. The geese pull me down. Somehow in falling I grip the puffed sleeve of her blouse and tear it from her shoulder.

There I am, on the ground, sprawled and burdened by the geese, clutching that sky-color bit of cloth. I think at first she will do me more damage with her shoes. But she just stands glaring down on me, rail-tough and pale as birch, her face loose and raging beneath the white cloth. I think that now the tears will spurt out. She will sob. But Marie is the kind of tree that doubles back and springs up, whips singing.

She bends over lightly and snatches the sleeve from my grip.

"Lay there, you ugly sonofabitch," she says.

I never answer, never say one word, just surge forward, knock her over, and roll on top of her and hold her pinned down underneath my whole length.

"Now we'll talk, skinny white girl, dirty Lazarre!" I yell in her face.

The geese are to my advantage now; their weight on my arms helps pin her; their dead wings flap around us; their necks loll, and their black eyes stare, frozen. But Marie is not the kind of girl to act frightened of a few dead geese.

She stares into my eyes, furious and silent, her lips clenched white.

"Just give me that pillowcase," I say, "and I'll let you go. I'm gonna bring that cloth back to the nuns."

She burns up at me with such fierceness, then, that I think she hasn't understood what a little thing I am asking. Her eyes are tense and wild, animal eyes. My neck chills.

"There now," I say in a more reasonable voice, "quit clutching it and I'll let you up and go. You shouldn't have stole it."

"Stole it!" she spits. "Stole!"

Her mouth drops wide open. If I want I could look all the way down her throat. Then she makes an odd raspfile noise, cawing like a crow.

She is laughing! It is too much. The Lazarre is laughing in my face!

"Stop that." I put my hand across her mouth. Her slick white teeth click, harmless, against my palm, but I am not satisfied.

"Lemme up," she mumbles.

"No," I say.

She lays still, then goes stiller. I look into her eyes and see the hard tears have frozen in the corners. She moves her legs. I keep her down. Something happens. The bones of her hips lock to either side of my hips, and I am held in a light vise. I stiffen like I am shocked. It hits me then I am lying full length across a woman, not a girl. Her breasts graze my chest, soft and pointed. I cannot help but lower myself the slightest bit to feel them better. And then I am caught. I give way. I cannot help myself, because to my everlasting wonder, Marie is all tight plush acceptance, graceful movements, little jabs that lead me underneath her skirt where she is slick, warm, silk. I touch her with one hand and in that one touch I lose myself.

When I come back, and when I look down on her, I know how badly I have been weakened. Her tongue flattens against my palm. I know that when I take my hand away the girl will smile, because somehow I have been beaten at what I started on this hill. And sure enough, when I take my hand away she growls.

"I've had better."

I know that isn't true because we haven't done anything yet. She just doesn't know what comes next. I can hear the shake in her voice, but that makes no difference. She still scares me. I scramble away from her, holding the geese in front. Although she is just a little girl knocked down in the dirt, she sits up, smooth as you please, fixes the black skirt over her knees, rearranges the pillowcase tied around her hand.

We are unsheltered by bushes. Anyone could have seen us. I glance around. On the hill, the windows dark in the white-washed brick seem to harbor a thousand holy eyes widening and narrowing.

How could I? It is then I panic, mouth hanging open, all but certain. They saw! I can hardly believe what I have done.

Marie is watching me. She sees me swing blind to the white face of the convent. She knows exactly what is going through my mind.

"I hope they saw it," she says in the crow's rasp.

I shut my mouth, then open it, then shut my mouth again. Who is this girl? I feel my breath failing like a stupid fish in the airless space around her. I lose control.

"I never did!" I shout, breaking my voice. I whirl to her. She is looking at the geese I hold in front to hide my shame. I speak wildly.

"You made me! You forced me!"

"I made you!" She laughs and shakes her hand, letting the pillowcase drop clear so that I can see the ugly wound.

"I didn't make you do anything," she says.

Her hand looks bad, cut and swollen, and it has not been washed. Even afraid as I am, I cannot help but feel how bad her hand must hurt and throb. Thinking this causes a small pain to shoot through my own hand. The girl's hand must have hurt when I threw her on the ground, and yet she didn't cry out. Her head, too. I have to wonder what is under the bandage. Did the nuns catch her and beat her when she tried to steal their linen?

The dead birds feel impossibly heavy. I untie them from my wrists and let them fall in the dirt. I sit down beside her.

"You can take these birds home. You can roast them," I say. "I am giving them to you."

Her mouth twists. She tosses her head and looks away.

I'm not ashamed, but there are some times this happens: alone in the woods, checking the trapline, I find a wounded animal that hasn't died well, or, worse, it's still living, so that I have to put it out of its misery. Sometimes it's just a big bird I only winged. When I do what I have to do, my throat swells closed sometimes. I touch the suffering bodies like they were killed saints I should handle with gentle reverence.

This is how I take Marie's hand. This is how I hold her wounded hand in my hand.

She never looks at me. I don't think she dares let me see her face. We sit alone. The sun falls down the side of the world and the hill goes dark. Her hand grows thick and fevered, heavy in my own, and I don't want her, but I want her, and I cannot let go.

The Magic Pony

GREG SARRIS

My name is Jasmine, but I'm no sweet-smelling flower. Names are just parents' dreams, after all. I'm thirty pounds too big and even more dull faced than my mother, since I make no effort to camouflage it with powder and lipstick. My cousin Ruby is pretty, but it's not the kind of pretty boys see. She's thin and clothes hang on her just so, like her mom, my Auntie Faye.

Us Indians are full of evil, Auntie Faye said. She told lots of stories about curses and poison. We call it poison. Not that we're bad people. Not like regular thieves and murderers. We inherit it. Something our ancestors did, maybe, or something we did to bring it on ourselves. Something we didn't realize—like having talked about somebody in a way they didn't like, so they got mad and poisoned you.

She knew a lot about poison. She said she had an

instinct for it. She'd nod with her chin to a grove of trees. "Don't walk there," she'd say. Her eyes looked dark and motionless, like she was seeing something she didn't want to see and couldn't look away from. She traced poison in a family. Take the receptionist at Indian Health, who has a black birthmark the size of a quarter on her cheek. Faye said the woman's mother stole something from someone, so the woman was marked from birth. It happens like that. It can circle around and get someone in your family. It's everywhere, Faye said.

Which is why she painted a forest on the front room wall and painted crosses over it with pink fingernail polish, to keep poison away. She wanted us to touch one of the crosses every day. "You'll be safe," she said.

I knew she was half cracked. I never believed any of her nonsense. I knew what Mom and my other aunts said was true: Faye had lost it. She was plumb nuts. And Ruby, who was fourteen, my age, wasn't far behind her. Ruby talked to extraterrestrials who landed on the street outside. She'd read books in the library and come out acting like some character in the book: Helen Keller or Joan of Arc or some proper English girl. She made no sense. Nothing about Ruby or Faye made sense, but I lived with them anyway.

I wasn't normal either.

I wanted to hear Auntie Faye's weird stories. I wanted to know what the extraterrestrials told Ruby. I wanted to sit at the kitchen table that Faye set each day with place mats and clean silverware and fresh flowers and hear nothing but their voices in the cool, quiet air of the room. I begged my mother. "Auntie Faye said I could live there," I told her. She looked at me as if I told her I had an extra eye in the back of my head. She knew me and Ruby were friendly, but she didn't think I'd go as far as wanting to live there. Seeing how shocked she was, I begged that much harder. I cried, threatened to run away. What could she say? She didn't have a place for us, not really. We lived with Grandma Zelda. Like all of my aunts and their kids when they get bounced out of their apartments for not paying the rent or something. Only Mom seemed permanent at Grandma Zelda's. She could never keep a place of her own for long.

Grandma Zelda's apartment is like the others, a no-color brown refurbished army barracks at the end of Grand Avenue. Grandma Zelda, Faye, my other aunts—all of us lived there. It was like our own reservation in Santa Rosa, just for our clan. Each apartment was full of the same stuff: dirty-diaper-smelling kids, hollering and fighting. But Grandma's place was the worst. It stunk twenty-four hours a day, and you never knew where you were going to sleep: on the floor, on the couch, in a chair. Babies slept in drawers. And then all the sounds in the dark. The crap with Mom and her men. And my aunts, too. All their moaning and stuff. All the time hoping none of it got close to you.

So you can see how Faye and Ruby's BS sounded to me like water trickling from a cool mountain stream, pleasure to the ears. It wasn't water that could drown you.

104

Sometimes it was even amusing. I'd guess how their stories would turn out because they got predictable. Of course Grandma Zelda and my other aunts were shocked when I carried my things to Faye's. I knew they wouldn't stop me, and they wouldn't come looking for me either. Faye's place was just two down from Grandma's, but it might as well have been in San Francisco, fifty miles away. No one hung around Faye's. If they came over, they'd stay half a second, then leave, like if they didn't get out fast enough they'd catch a disease. I was safe.

Then Auntie Faye found a man, and one day me and Ruby came home from school and found Mom and all our aunts at Faye's like it was a everyday thing.

Billyrene. Pauline. Rita. Stella. Mom. Even Grandma Zelda. All of them were there putting on a show. Big, dull-faced Indian women with assorted hair colors. They fooled with their hair and tugged at their blouses, each one hoping Faye's man would take notice. Each one had her own plan to get the man for herself. I know Mom and my aunts. Nothing stops them when they get ideas, and nothing gives them ideas like a man does. First the lollipop-sweet smiles and phony shyness, then the cattiness, the sharp words. By the time Ruby and me got there, they had their claws out.

"Did you come from the mission?" Grandma Zelda asked the man, who sat next to Faye on the couch.

He didn't seem to hear her. Maybe he was overwhelmed by the line of beauties that surrounded him. Me and Ruby stood pushed up against the wall. No one saw us, not even Faye, who was looking in our direction. Her eyes weren't strange. They weren't still. She looked back and forth as people talked. I felt funny all of a sudden. I'd seen the man before. There was nothing to him, I saw that right off. He was white, ugly, orange-colored, with thick hairy arms and eyes that were little blue stones, plastic jewelry in a junk shop. It wasn't him that bothered me, really. It was Faye, the way she followed the conversation, and Mom and all them in the room. My stomach slid like a tire on an icy road.

"Did you come from the mission?" Grandma asked again. She was the only one in a dress, an old lady print, with her stained yellow slip hanging to her ankles.

"What kind of question is that?" Mom snapped. She smiled at Faye's man, as if telling him not to pay any attention to the idiot old woman.

"Frances," Grandma said, "all I meant was is he Christian?"

Faye laughed, trying to make light of all the talk. She gently elbowed her man to let him know to laugh too.

I turned to Ruby. With all that was going on in front of her, her eyes were a million miles away. It aggravated me that she stood there in never-never land. I grabbed her arm and whispered, "That man's going to be your new father."

She didn't focus, so I said it again, this time loud and clear.

"That man's going to be your new father."

Grandma Zelda looked in our direction. "Hush up,"

she snapped. She didn't really see me and Ruby. We could've been Rita's three-year-old twins for all she knew. She didn't hear what I said either. No one did.

Then Billyrene piped up, Billyrene in her aqua stretch pants and a white blouse that didn't cover her protruding belly. "Lord knows Faye don't meet men in the mission. Not like some people here." She was looking straight at Mom and Pauline and Rita, giving them an evil gap-toothed smile.

On and on it went. Then out came the beer. They drank awhile, then left. Faye and her man went with them.

I hadn't cooked a meal since I left Grandma Zelda's eight months before. Even with this guy in Faye's life, she hadn't missed cooking for me and Ruby until that night. Tuna casserole, that's what I ended up making, just like I used to for everybody at Grandma's. Ruby set the table. We ate and didn't say anything to each other. Not until we were doing the dishes. I was washing, she was drying. I was thinking about Faye and Mom and my aunts, all their catty talk. Faye would laugh, but she had to know how bad it can get, especially if they're drinking. If they don't beat on one another, they'll go after somebody else. Like the time Pauline and Mom got into it over who used all the gas in Pauline's pickup. They were hollering at each other in Cherri's Chinese Kitchen. Cherri, the owner, tried to settle them down, and Mom hit her over the head with a Coke bottle. The cops came and took Mom, the whole thing. I was picturing all that when I looked at Ruby, who was drying dishes calm as you please. She might as well have been standing next to a sink on the moon. "Your mother's crazy," I blurted out. "She's a freak and so are you."

She finished wiping a plate and placed it in the cupboard. Then she reached for another plate from the dish rack.

"Did you hear me?" I yelled. My aggravation had turned into pure pissed-off. She paid no attention to me. "Damn you, you freak!" I cupped my hand into the sink and splashed her with the hot, dirty dishwater. She was stunned. The dishwater hit her in the face, all over the front of her. But she did just what you'd expect. She got a hold on herself. She dried the plate, even soaking wet as she was, and set it in the cupboard. Then she put down the towel and walked away.

She got out the Monopoly board. She wanted me to sit down and play with her. Whenever I got upset, like with my flunking-out grades at school, she opened the Monopoly board. She cheated so I could win. She wanted me to feel better. I knew what she was up to, but I didn't say anything. I looked at her, sitting on the couch, waiting, soaking wet. I turned, picked up the towel, and finished the dishes she was drying.

The man's name was Jerry. Where Auntie Faye found him I'm not sure. The grocery store, I think. When I first saw him come into the house with her, he was carrying a bag of groceries. He was nothing special, like I said. White, ugly. He'd come each afternoon and visit with Faye. He'd come around three, about the time me and Ruby got home from school, and leave at five, when Faye started cooking supper. He always brought something: flowers, a can of coffee, a pair of candles. It went on like that for a couple weeks, until the day Mom and my aunts came into the house and him and Faye left with them.

I knew Faye was lonely. She had bad luck with men. Ruby's father died in a car crash on his way to the hospital the night Ruby was born. He had been over in Graton drinking. But Faye didn't see it that way. She said she was cursed for loving his brother first. The brother's name was Joaquin. He got killed in the Vietnam War. Six months later Faye married Ruby's father. From the way she talked, I don't think she ever stopped loving Joaquin. She never dated after Ruby's father died. I know because I used to hear Mom and my aunts go on in that dirty woman-talk way about Faye not having a man, and until Jerry came I never saw a guy near the place. It wasn't that Faye couldn't get a man. Just the opposite. She didn't look like Mom and my aunts. She wasn't heavy, plain-looking. She was slender and wore clothes like a lady in a magazine. Everything just so, even the dark pants and white blouse she wore around the house.

But Faye's loneliness was about more than not having a man. It was bigger, more than about Joaquin and what happened to Ruby's father. I saw it in her eyes when me and Ruby left each morning for school. Her eyes got wide, not really focusing on me and Ruby but just staring. She'd be sitting at the table, plates of toast and half-empty bowls of cereal all around, and from the door, where me and Ruby said good-bye, she looked so small, sitting there dressed just so.

When she told stories about poison, she looked lonely, scared. She'd sit me and Ruby at the table and tell us what certain pink crosses on her painting meant. She had painted the big green forest first, the dark trunks and thick green leaves, then kept adding crosses here and there with fingernail polish, a pink color she never used on herself. Each cross had a story of its own. When she talked, her eyes narrowed. They seemed to squeeze like two hands trying to hold on to something. It was always about what happened to somebody, like the one about our Cousin Jeanne's Old Uncle. It's why Jeanne and them don't live in the barracks with us, why they split off from the family a long time ago, when everybody was still on the reservation. Her Old Uncle—I guess he's our Old Uncle too— liked this woman from Clear Lake, but she was married. He liked her so much he put a spell on her husband. Old Uncle could do things like that, poison people. But the poison turned on him. Something happened. It got his sister. One night she was playing blackjack; the next morning she was as cold and still as a rock in winter. That's how our great-aunt died, Faye said. She held a pointing stick, the kind teachers use with a rubber tip, and aimed near the center of the painting. "And it's why your Cousin Jeanne has cancer," she told us. "She inherited it. His misuse of power, it's living yet."

When she talked about Ruby's father or Joaquin, she pointed to a cross near the bottom of the forest, on the right-hand side. "Man sickness," she said. "Man poison."

Somehow because of that cross and the way she talked about it, I figured she'd never have a boyfriend. Maybe she thought she was poisoned when it came to men, so she'd never have one. After Jerry started coming, she stood by the painting with her fingers on that cross and whispered, "Oh, Father, help against this poison. Keep me safe from it. Don't let it turn on me." I couldn't hear her, but I knew what she said. If me and Ruby got the urge to steal something, we had to say these words and touch the cross with the stealing story. If someone wanted to hurt us, beat us up for something, we had a cross for that, too.

I never thought much about Faye praying on the man-sickness cross until after Jerry and Faye left with Mom and them that day. Jerry started coming around more, not just in the afternoons but late at night, after supper, and Mom and my aunts visited more and more. I thought about my own words, what I said to Ruby that day about the ugly man becoming her new father. Faye told me more than once I had a mean mouth sometimes and I should watch what I say. Never mind that her daughter made up the tallest tales on earth. She never said nothing about that. I don't remember if there was a cross for me to touch regarding my mean teasing mouth; what I said turned out true. The man moved in.

Me and Ruby moved out of the bedroom where we used to sleep on the bed with Faye. Now we slept on the couch, with our heads at opposite ends. "You can camp out on the couch," Faye said one night, as if it were something we had asked to do and she was letting us. Our legs met in the middle, and every time one of us moved or turned we got kicked. I thought of Faye in the bed with Jerry. The door was closed. I couldn't hear anything. Still, I couldn't sleep. I tried squeezing my eyes shut, but I kept seeing Faye with Jerry, disgusting things. Either way, with my eyes opened or closed, everything was dark, a perfect empty backdrop for all I was seeing in my mind. I looked to the painting above us, over the couch. The crosses glowed faintly in the light coming through the front window. "Ruby," I whispered, "maybe your dumb mother can find a cross that'll get us a bed."

Of course she didn't answer me. I sat up and looked at her. She was awake, staring, the window light in her eyes. I knew she heard me.

"Damn you," I said, and yanked the blankets off her. She didn't move. She was probably in deep communication with a Martian that was signaling her from the back side of the barracks. Hours later I was still awake. Ruby was asleep. I sat up and covered her with the blankets. I woke up that way in the morning, sitting up.

Faye didn't pray at her painting anymore. She dusted it with her feather duster the way she dusted the top of the TV. She'd remind us to think of the crosses when we left for school each morning, but that's about all. No more stories about poison and what can happen to people. No more holding hands after one of the stories, which is what we always did. She'd finish the story, put down her pointing stick, and then we'd hold hands over the table while she said the prayer about Father God helping us against the poison.

Now she talked about ordinary stuff. The ladies she knew at the cannery. Specials at the grocery store. What was in the window at the secondhand shop on Fifth Street. She talked about getting a new place, a house someplace where me and Ruby could have our own bedroom, maybe even out of Santa Rosa. She had it planned. She wasn't going to work at the cannery anymore, where she was laid off half the year. She was going to be a nurse's aide in a convalescent hospital. Jerry knew someone who could get her a job. Once she talked about tenderness, its merits; it makes people smile, she said. It makes them have faith in others. It makes people feel connected. Then she threw her head back and dropped her shoulders, like she'd got goose bumps all of a sudden. "It's like a light's inside you." Jerry was there, and I felt embarrassed, like I was hearing what I didn't want to imagine seeing behind the bedroom door at night.

Jerry was always there, since he was out of work. Temporarily, Faye said. He helped Faye with the shopping and stuff and he still brought her things, flowers and once a coffee mug with red hearts on it. Lots about him bugged me. Like the way he chewed his food. He mashed it, curling his lips out so you could see the food in his mouth. He asked if me and Ruby were cheerleaders. That was funny. I wanted to ask him if he thought we looked like cheerleaders.

113

But I didn't.

Faye was happy these days. She used to get moody sometimes, just stare into space, and she'd snap at you if you talked to her. Now she was always up, and just by the way she acted you knew she wanted everybody else up too. She'd look at you and there was something in her eyes, something behind the brightness, that was scary. You wouldn't want to cross her. Seemed like Mom and my aunts saw this in Faye's eyes, too. They came to the house almost every day now; there was none of their bitchy talk. Everybody was nice, the way Faye wanted. Her and Mom and Grandma went on and on about how they could help Pauline get her two younger kids out of juvenile hall. Stuff like that. It made me nervous. I know my aunts. There was something behind their niceness, something like what I saw in Faye's eyes.

Me and Ruby spent more and more time doing things. It was toward the end of the school year. The days were longer. We took walks. We'd go to the fairgrounds, up to the slaughterhouse on Santa Rosa Avenue, and even to the mall. Anywhere except the library, which I couldn't stand. I'd put up with anything, her stories about extraterrestrials, anything to keep her head out of a book. That's why I got caught up in the horse thing, the magic pony.

It was a regular horse, a small pinto gelding, not much bigger than a pony. She called it a pony. It was at the slaughterhouse with the other horses. One of the things me and Ruby did those days was sit in the rusted-out boxcar by the slaughterhouse and watch the horses. She had them all named: King Tut, Cleopatra, Romeo and Juliet, the Duke of Earl. We didn't talk about what happened to them when the owner took them from the front corral, where we watched them, to the back corral: a loud buzzer, then the gun blast. Sometimes the horses got lucky. If they were gentle and sound, rich people bought them for their kids.

One day this pony darted out from a group of bigger horses by the trough. He was munching a mouthful of hay, and he kept running here and there, snatching hay from the troughs. He moved so fast the others didn't see him. After a while he walked to the cement tub by the fence for a drink. That's when Ruby flew off the boxcar to pet him. True, he lifted his head and whinnied at her. He probably would have done that for me if I had gotten there first. But Ruby didn't see it that way. He communicated with *her*.

That night in bed I heard everything. Far as she was concerned, the pony wasn't black and white but pure silver and gold. A horse who never drank water. He lived off the morning dew and the pollen of spring flowers. A magic pony that carried princesses into fields of poppies and purple lupine. He soared on wind currents over this town with wings stretched wide as an eagle's. He told Ruby he needed a home.

Faye and Jerry were gone, out with Mom and them. I was trying to sleep. I didn't want to be awake when they got home. Ruby wouldn't quit this horse business. "Shut up," I finally said.

Strange thing, though, the horse could do tricks. We went to the slaughterhouse every day. Before long Ruby was in the corral with it, riding it and everything. Smoke, the owner, a tall black man, gave her a bridle. Even he was surprised to see the pony back up and kneel down on command. He let Ruby take the pony into the open field across the street, where the last flowers of spring were blooming, poppies and lupine. He said the pony might've been in the circus. He didn't know much, except the man who dropped the pony off said it had foundered. "Too bad," he said. When he told me this, we were leaning on the fence watching Ruby and the pony in the field. His words fell like dust and piled on my shoulders. I didn't know what foundered was, but I looked back to Ruby just then, and in the early evening light, she seemed to be floating, nothing holding her as she glided above the dried oat grass and flowers.

I told her to forget the pony. I opened her dictionary and pointed to the word *founder*. "Nobody's going to want that pony," I said. "You know what's going to happen." I expected her to argue with me, to point out that the stiffness in the pony's front legs was barely noticeable. But she didn't. She took the dictionary from me, set it on the table, and said matter-of-factly, "That's why he told me he needed a home. I have to find him one."

She couldn't think of anything else. Day and night she figured and planned. For two weeks she approached everybody who came to the slaughterhouse, telling them how the pony was magic. She'd jump on its back, without a bridle, and show folks how well trained he was. The pony would back up and kneel with just a little tug on its mane. By this time Ruby could get the pony to do anything. People watched, young pretty-looking girls and white shirt-and-tie fathers. They'd clap, cheer Ruby on, but they always ended up looking at other horses. Finally it occurred to Ruby what I had been telling her all along. Smoke told people about the pony's legs.

Then she went to Jerry, which was the dumbest idea ever. "If he's my father now, he can help me get the pony," she said. Jerry didn't have a pot to piss in, for as things turned out he was living off Auntie Faye's unemployment from the cannery, just like me and Ruby. The flowers he brought Faye he picked out of people's gardens, and the other things, like the coffee mug, he found in trash bins or stole from garage sales. One morning I saw him pocket me and Ruby's lunch money. I didn't tell Faye. I feared that person I had seen behind her happy eyes. But I told Ruby. I reminded her of that and of Jerry's money problems. She didn't listen.

"I want the pony," she told him one night.

He was sitting at the kitchen table, having a beer with Faye and Mom. It was late, after supper. I watched from the couch that I had just covered with a sheet and blankets for bed. Ruby stood only a couple feet from Jerry, determined. Jerry didn't answer her. He seemed surprised, as if he had looked up and seen Ruby for the first time.

"Ruby," Faye said. "You know we're moving soon. That takes extra money. Jerry and me are saving. Wait until after we move." Her voice was muffled, far away, like a seagull calling over crashing waves. I noticed she sounded like this when she drank.

Ruby looked straight at Jerry. "I want the pony."

Mom took a swallow of beer and set down her bottle. "Ruby," she said, "you should talk it over with Grandma. She could help maybe from her Social Security check." Mom acted as if she were really interested. She thought she was important these days since she'd found a job at a convalescent hospital.

Jerry, who was still looking at Ruby as if he didn't know her, turned suddenly to Mom. "Your mother's old," he said. "She needs her money." He looked at Ruby. "Go to one of the farmers around here."

Ruby was up against a wall. Finally she quit. She came back and sat on the cot next to the couch. Later, after Mom left and Faye and Jerry went in the bedroom, she said, "See, Jerry did help me. He told me what to do." She was lying on top of the cot, still dressed. She stared at the ceiling, already seeing a thin Indian girl with long straight hair standing before a farmer's open front door.

We walked five miles down Petaluma Hill Road to the dairies. We went to front doors and into noisy milk barns and smelly calf pens, looking for farmers who might want the pony. Ruby never said hello. She didn't introduce herself. "There's this pony," she'd say, and go on and on. Most people let her finish before they asked us to leave. One farmer was interested. He was a fat, whiskered man in dirty pants that hung halfway down his white ass. He signaled us to follow him so he could hear us over the loud milking machines in that barn where he and two Mexican men milked enormous black-and-white cows. We went into a dark, windowless room. Metal pipes fed a huge shiny tank, where they kept the milk. The farmer leaned against the wall and folded his hands over his belly. His fingers were thick and hairy.

"You can see him at the slaughterhouse," Ruby said.

"What's wrong with him? Gotta be something wrong with him," the man said. I didn't like the way he took time between his words, and I felt his eyes on Ruby, though I didn't look. I grabbed her hand and gauged my distance from the door.

Ruby took her time answering him. "He needs a home," she finally said. "He gets around good, and he can get up and down with me on him."

The man told us his daughter wanted a horse. Then he said, "I'll go look at him. Meet me back here next week, same time."

I yanked Ruby out the door.

On the way to the main road, we passed a farmhouse where a girl about ten years old stood watering a vegetable garden.

"See, Jerry was right," Ruby said.

"At least he has a daughter," I said. "I still think he's a pervert."

I knew Ruby wouldn't listen to me, but I didn't like the idea of us going back to that dairy. I didn't like that dark room. I felt trapped.

It's not that I hate men. I just know them too well. I've been around Mom and my aunts and seen what they bring home. I've seen it all. The stuff that goes on in the dark, the stuff you're not supposed to know about but end up seeing anyway. Like when I saw Auntie Pauline's man pulling off my cousin Angela's pants in Pauline's pickup, Pauline's daughter who's my age, the one in juvee. Or when that guy Armando hit Auntie Rita in the chest. Or Tito, Mom's last man: the way he tried to get at me at night when Mom was asleep. You develop a sixth sense for it. You see things you don't want to see. You run right into it. It isn't always something heavy like with Pauline's man and Angela. It can be something simple, innocent looking.

Like the way Mom and Jerry were sitting in Pauline's pickup outside the supermarket. You could say there were a lot of groceries on the seat, or maybe a dog or a child that caused them to have to sit so close together. You knew, though, that they could have put a dog or a child between them. But it's more than their sitting that way; it's something about them that is still, something about the way they quietly turn their faces to each other, Mom looking up so that her eyes meet his, that tells you the whole story, not just in this moment but in all of those in the dark, where Faye hadn't seen them. And you can hear the excuse: "Jerry and me are picking up some things at the store."

I watched them from behind a car in the parking lot. First I saw Pauline's pickup, the red Toyota, then the back of Mom's head, her teased orange-red hair that was supposed to be blond. I knew the whole story even before I had time to think about it. My stomach turned. I wanted to heave. I started up Milton toward Grand. I yanked my hair just so the pain would take my mind off things. It wasn't that I was shocked by Mom and Jerry or the things people do, sex and all that. I was worried about what was going to happen at home.

Already things were nuts. Faye's place was no different now from Grandma Zelda's or Pauline's. Me and Ruby ate canned soup on the couch for dinner. In the mornings we made our own toast and poured our own cornflakes, since Faye didn't get up with us anymore. The door stayed closed, locked. Ruby did nothing but obsess over the pony. She didn't even do her schoolwork now. I couldn't talk to her. Her eyes were like a pair of headlights on the highway, staring straight ahead, zooming past me. She spent all her time at the slaughterhouse, waiting to see if the farmer or anyone else came to see the pony and making sure Smoke didn't move him to the back, behind the white barn. "The farmer could come while we're in school," I said. But she wouldn't budge. She wouldn't leave the pony's side. The afternoon I saw Mom and Jerry in Pauline's pickup, I had left her braiding the pony's scraggly mane.

When I got a hold of my senses, I thought of telling Ruby. I was sitting on Grandma Zelda's porch step. I had come to Faye's first, but when I got to the open screen door and heard all the folks yapping inside, I continued along the row of barracks to Grandma's and plunked myself down. I could hear the loud laughter at Faye's two doors away.

It was a couple of hours before Ruby came up the path at twilight. I jumped up and ran to meet her, feeling desperate to let out everything in my swelled brain. But I ended up saying nothing. I stopped, seeing her face as she turned to go inside, and knew that if I told her what I had seen, her eyes would only look harder and move away from me.

In the days ahead I wanted to talk to Ruby, not just about Mom and Jerry. The weather would have been enough to carry on about, far as I was concerned. But nothing. No way. I'm one to shout, shake her up with what I say, but I could've screamed at the top of my lungs and it would've done as much good as trying to stop a hundred-mile-an-hour train with a whisper. I couldn't stand being in the house. I wanted to kill Mom while she sat nice as could be talking to Auntie Faye. I wanted to pour gasoline on Jerry and watch him burn to black ashes. I stuck by Ruby. I lived at the slaughterhouse with her. But it seemed to make no difference. I was alone.

We went back to the dairy after a week, just like the farmer said, same time. "We're not going in that back room," I said. But there was no need to worry. The farmer must've seen us coming up the road. He met us in front of the milk barn. He pulled up his sagging pants, then adjusted his stained green cap to cover his eyes.

"That little Indian pony," he said, "I went and seen him. I don't know what you girls was thinking. He's useless."

Of course Faye would find out about Mom and Jerry. For me waiting was like standing on a tightrope, not knowing when I'd fall or where I'd land when I did. I didn't have to wait long. On the last day of school, after me and Ruby got home at noon, Faye explained everything.

Suddenly things were back to the old routine. Faye was sitting at the kitchen table with her pointing stick. She motioned with her chin for me and Ruby to sit down. She was plain looking again, pale like she was before she'd met Jerry. Her eyes were distant, preoccupied. The table was set, with flowers in a mayonnaise jar. When she lifted her pointing stick to gesture at the painting on the wall, I saw she had drawn circles around many of the crosses and connected them with lines from one to another. She had used what looked like a black crayon.

She pointed to the cross circled near the bottom of the painting. "Man sickness," she reminded us, and got up and went to the painting. "Man poison." She looked to Ruby. "Your father and also Joaquin, his brother. I loved Joaquin first."

She followed a line that connected this cross to one that was circled near the center of the painting. She was straightforward, a history teacher giving a lecture for the hundredth time.

"This one here," she said, now looking at both of us, "is Old Uncle's poison. Misuse of power. Do you see how they connect here?"

I sat motionless.

"I'll tell you," she said. She let her pointer hang by her side. "This is what happened. You know I loved Joaquin first. Isn't that right?"

We nodded in agreement.

"You know I loved him. Yes, but I never should have." She paused and swallowed hard, color coming to her pale cheeks. "I stole him from your cousin Jeanne's mother, Anna. I stole him from Anna. I stole him in the worst way. I plotted with my sisters, your aunts, Billyrene and Pauline. We embarrassed her. We told Joaquin that Anna was poison because she and her mother lived with Old Uncle, who poisoned our aunt. It worked. It split them up. Anna and her mother disappeared. We didn't see them for many years, until we moved here. But that's not the point. What really happened is that Old Uncle's poison found me. Misuse of power. I opened a hole in my heart, and it found a place to live."

She took a deep breath and pushed back her hair with her free hand. "I killed two men." She pointed to the two circled crosses and traced the line between them, back and forth. "Each man I love I kill. Each man I touch because the poison in me does that. Now my own sisters are full of the poison. It's growing in them, and they're using it against me. They plotted and took Jerry."

Faye walked over and set the pointing stick on the table. "Now drink your orange juice," she said.

I heard her push the toaster down behind us and I smelled the toast. But it wasn't until I saw the buttered toast on the table that I realized how far Faye had gone with her story. Things weren't back to normal. Faye had gone off the edge. "Now hurry or you'll be late for school," she said.

Later that day I followed Ruby to the slaughterhouse to try and talk to her. "Look," I said, "this is serious. Your mother's nuts." Ruby had hardly said a word to me the whole week. "Listen to me," I said. We were standing just outside the corral. "Damn you, you stupid fool, wake up."

She slipped through the board fence to where the pony was waiting for her. Its white ears were perked up and it whinnied, just as it did every time it saw Ruby. She stroked its neck and led it to the front of the corral, by the main road where passersby could see them. The buzzer went off in the white barn; then I heard it, a gunshot. I climbed over the fence and made my way past the bigger horses to Ruby and the pony. She had her arms around its neck, tightly, and its head was over her shoulder facing my direction.

"Okay," I said. "I'm sorry. Anyway, it's my stupid mother's fault. I'm sorry." I don't know how many times I said it. But she never turned around. Even the pony ignored me, never perked up its ears. I felt like a fifth wheel. Like I had no business there in the little world that was all their own.

Faye got her time straight, a good sign. When me and Ruby got home, after dark, she scolded us for staying out so late. "Dinner's cold," she said. She was truly angry. She shoved the food she had prepared into the oven and slammed the stove door shut. Ten minutes later me and

Ruby were sitting at a table set with flowers, eating pork chops, fresh green beans, and a baked potato with sour cream, my favorite. Ruby talked on and on about the pony, crazy stuff about how it could fly and disappear, and Faye forgot about us being late.

When we finished eating, Faye went to the painting and so did Ruby. Faye wiped her mouth with her folded paper napkin and then got up, and Ruby followed her, as if Faye wiping her mouth was a signal. How else did Ruby know what Faye was doing? Usually Faye went and stood by her painting before dinner or in the morning or early afternoon. Then I saw Ruby's eyes. Walking to the painting, she looked back at me. She looked at me so I knew she was looking, and I felt like I did earlier with her hugging the pony. Only I felt worse now; I saw more, even after she looked away and joined Faye, starting in on Father God for help. I saw that Ruby wasn't in never-never land. She was always here. She was always aware of me next to her. Faye was okay too. How could she not know how hard her life had been and that my mother, her sister, had just stolen her man? Ruby knew and Faye knew, just like me. But they believed in something—Faye her crosses, Ruby the pony—and I didn't. I clung to them, and they let me.

We slept together that night. Faye told stories about when she was a girl living on the reservation. She told us the Indian names of flowers. She told us about wild birds. "*Cita*," she said. "Bird. *Cita, cita*." I fell asleep and must've slept hard because I woke up late, without Faye or Ruby.

I went to the front room, and just as if it had jumped out at me, I saw Faye's painting—or what was left of it—before I even saw Faye. It was black, totally black, the color she had circled the crosses with the day before. Black, except for the edges here and there where you could see a bit of green from the trees underneath. It was as if I were waking up just then, as if in the bedroom I hadn't been awake at all. The fragile peace I had felt shattered like thin glass into a million pieces.

I turned to Faye, who was sitting at the table. Nothing was set, no breakfast dishes, nothing, and the flowers from the mayonnaise jar were laid out around a butcher knife, a halo of green and yellow and purple around the silver blade.

"Faye," I said. "Auntie Faye."

She didn't look at me but kept staring at the painting. It took a minute, and then she started talking. "I must kill Frances—"

"My mother?" I asked.

"I must kill Frances. Otherwise she'll kill Jerry. She's full of poison. She'll kill Jerry. Tonight I will kill her. She is hate. The poison is hate."

"Auntie Faye," I called, but she didn't see me.

I realized talking about it was useless when I saw her eyes. The fearful person I had seen behind her bright eyes the past few weeks had come out now; she was that person. She had told stories to save herself—now she was telling them to excuse herself. Hatred. Jealousy. Anger. Evil. All I had seen in my mother's and my aunts' eyes at different times was here in Faye's. I looked back at the black wall, where Faye was looking, then ran out of the house.

I went to the slaughterhouse. Ruby wasn't there, so I ran through the corral and shouted up into the hay barn, where the horses were eating. I hollered and hollered. Nothing. Only the yellow bales of hay stared at me. I went around the back, behind the big white barn across from the front corral, and that's when I spotted the pony. He was there along with a crippled bay mare standing on three legs, a few unshorn sheep, and an emaciated white-face cow. A large eucalyptus tree shaded the cramped pen. "Ruby!" I hollered. "Ruby!"

Smoke appeared in the door above the chute. "She ain't been around here today," he said. "Ain't seen her. Now get, you shouldn't be back here."

First I thought Ruby had run away. But that wasn't like her. I figured she had seen how the pony was in the back. Any day could be its last. Ruby wouldn't give up. She wouldn't run. She'd work harder. She'd go back to the dairies. She'd go farther down Petaluma Hill Road, all the way to Petaluma.

So that's what I did—went back to every dairy we had stopped at, asking everybody along the way if they had seen her. I made up stories, like she needed medicine. I described her, but no one had seen such a girl. I walked clear back to town. One last place, the library—but no luck. The only place left was Faye's.

Faye hadn't moved. All afternoon while I'd been running back and forth to the slaughterhouse looking for

Ruby and checking to see if the pony was alive, Faye never looked away from her painting to see me coming and going. I slammed the door. Once I even shook the table. I thought of reaching for the knife, but it was too close to Faye. She might snap, and I'd be within her reach.

I plunked myself down on the couch, and as the afternoon wore on I began hating Ruby. She had abandoned me. Faye was worse than useless. She was worse than gone. I thought of running over to Grandma Zelda's and telling her or Mom. But then what? Have them come down and get stabbed? I thought of calling the police, but why start trouble when it hadn't started? I guess, too, that I didn't want anyone to see Faye like this. They would take her away. I waited and waited. I wanted Ruby to come home, for things to be fine. Maybe Faye would flip back to her old self, I thought, if I just waited.

Faye must have gotten up so quietly I didn't notice. She was standing at the kitchen table looking toward the screen door. Slowly, deliberately, she walked to the door and stopped. "Jasmine," she said, "come here." Her voice was cool, even.

I went to the door.

"A miracle," she said.

And then I saw the sky, where Faye was looking. It was lit by a huge ball of fire, yellow, purple, golden, and red. I was stunned by the sight of it. Then I heard the sirens, and before I could think, I knew. Ruby had set the barn on fire.

I tore past Faye, around the crowds gathered outside

the barracks. I ran up Santa Rosa Avenue, past the flashing lights. Horses were everywhere, all over the street, stopping traffic, halting police cars and fire trucks. I was stopped by police and yellow tape, but in the thick of lights and uniforms, through the haze of smoke, I saw a plain-looking girl being escorted to a police van.

There was nothing to do but go back and tell what happened. There was nothing to hide now. I felt heavy, tired. The first people I saw were Auntie Pauline and my cousins. They were standing on Grand. Then I went in and told Faye. "I know," she said. "I know." She was sitting on the couch.

Funny thing, no one asked me how I knew it was Ruby. Everybody collected in Faye's. They waited for the police car. Something my family always does when there's trouble—wait together. Wait for the details. Auntie Pauline. Auntie Billyrene. Grandma Zelda. Auntie Rita. Mom and Jerry. Auntie Stella.

As it turned out, there wasn't a lot to the story. Ruby had opened the gates and then set the hay barn on fire. She let the horses go. Of course I was the only one who understood the details. I don't mean about how she hid out and poured gasoline on the hay and all that, which we found out later, after she was released from juvee and came back to Faye's. I mean about why she did it. What led up to it. I understood it plain as day even while I was sitting there next to Faye, waiting with everybody else for the police to come with Ruby.

There was nothing I could do. Faye was a crying mess

on the couch, and the cops had Ruby. Face it. Face reality, which I always did, which I told myself I should never have stopped doing. I had been hiding at Faye's. With her and Ruby I had been fooling myself. See the road ahead, I kept saying inside my brain. But when I saw Ruby come through the door, a uniformed policeman on each side of her, I stopped. My heart turned and never righted back.

"Jasmine," she blurted out, seeing me. "He's free. He flew away."

I said what made no sense. I said it like a prayer. "Everything's going to be all right, Ruby."

Summer Wind

LEE FRANCIS

It was a hot summer day when the Storyteller came to
our village. All I wanted to do was stay inside and watch
TV or chill to some tunes on my stereo. My granma had
something else in mind; I had to help her prepare for the
Storyteller's big event that night. Because it was my
granma, I did what she wanted without complaining. I set
up the chairs and card tables that I had borrowed from
everyone in the village. Then I gathered wood for the
campfire.

The old people, adults, and little kids were busy getting the campfire ready for the Storyteller's performance.
Apparently he was going to do his thing standing under
the old oak tree. Everyone was excited and acted as if his
visit were a spectacular event or a holiday. I couldn't care
less.

I had just finished my chores when this old guy drove

toward us in a dirty yellow 1970s Chevy Silverado pickup. He turned off the engine and got out. Within minutes the community surrounded him. They were shaking his hand, telling him how glad they were that he had come.

My granma came up to me and asked why I didn't join the others. I told her it was no big deal. She shrugged and said, "Suit yourself." Then she rushed to the old man and greeted him.

My granma was polite to everyone. I thought all that polite stuff was garbage. But don't misunderstand. I love my granma. She is my best friend. Actually, my only friend. Most of the kids my age are a bunch of jerks as far as I'm concerned. With Granma, I can be myself. Mostly the two of us just hang out. She doesn't fuss about what I watch on TV. Occasionally, though, she will ask why I'm watching a show that isn't, in her opinion, at all interesting. I explain that it's a great story. Granma smiles like she knows something, but she doesn't say a word. We have an understanding. If I don't ask, she won't tell. So I don't ask. I figure she'll let me in on what she knows if it's important. Truth is, Granma is smart, even if she acts like she isn't. An example: A couple of days ago we went to the grocery store. There was a new cashier at the checkout stand who had a real attitude. She rolled her eyes when Granma started putting the stuff we got on the counter. Then in a snotty tone of voice she announced the total: twelve dollars and twenty-seven cents. Granma smiled politely and then went into super slo-mo. She took her wallet from her handbag. That took at least two minutes. Then she opened her wallet and started counting out the change. I knew she had a twenty-dollar bill. I didn't smirk. My granma was, as she would say, helping someone learn. I think what she was helping the cashier learn was to not mess with her.

First Granma counted out ten dollars in quarters. That took a couple of minutes because she accidentally dropped a few on the floor. Granma and I picked them up and she started counting all over again. Then she stopped and looked at the cashier, who was really pissed. Granma asked the cashier to repeat the total. I wanted to burst out laughing, but I kept a straight face. Granma was really getting her money's worth. She continued counting out the change. Very slowly. Finally, after about eight minutes or so, she handed the change to the cashier, who by now was so mad that she dropped the coins. Quarters went flying all over the counter. I almost lost it. I could tell my granma was having a hard time not laughing too.

When the cashier had all the change in hand, Granma said that maybe she should count it again, with a polite smile. "Just to make sure it's all there." The cashier shook her head and said that it wouldn't be necessary. She handed Granma the receipt as I picked up the plastic bag filled with groceries. Then Granma told the cashier to have a nice day. Man, oh man, was that cashier furious. I heard her say real soft, "Damn Injuns." I pretended to not hear her. She reminded me of the jerks at school.

After we left the grocery store, I burst out laughing.

Granma joined me with a chuckle all her own. Then she got real serious. Glancing at me, she said that what she had done was not very nice. I looked solemn and agreed, and then we both started laughing again.

When I told Granma what the cashier had said, she looked real sad. She said the cashier was a pathetic soul and explained that people who do name-calling don't have any self-esteem. Like I said, when something is important, Granma tells me about it.

I guess you could say we're buddies. She can put someone in his place without batting an eye. Even me. That's why I didn't say anything about helping her prepare for the Storyteller's visit. I knew if I copped an attitude, we would get into it . . . and I would lose.

Finally we were all sitting around the old oak tree eating potluck. Everyone was talking softly. Now and again I could hear the voice of the Storyteller. He was speaking to people at each of the card tables. When he sat down at a table that I had set up just for him, it was sunset.

The wind started up. Granma called it summer wind. For her it was a sign of good things to come. I wasn't so sure. I mean, how could a wind, whether it was in the summer or winter, bring good things? Or even bad? When I asked Granma, she just shrugged and smiled knowingly.

I looked at everyone sitting by the oak tree. The summer wind cooled the air down quickly. One of the old men of the village got up and started the campfire. Granma and I were sitting pretty close to it. When the fire reached a quiet glow, the Storyteller stood up from the card table, where he had been eating his meal. He began to tell a story.

"And so. It is said among the People, in the long ago time, all of creation, seen and unseen, first existed as a tightly compacted single ball. After a long time had passed, Spider managed to crawl outside the ball.

"Outside the ball of creation there were no stars or light of any kind. There was only an incredibly small pinpoint of light coming from within the ball. It was the place from which Spider had crawled out. But Spider could not crawl back in. Spider became very lonely. Then Spider had an idea. What if it were possible to make a web? After I make a web, thought Spider, I must think of a way to loosen the tight ball. When I have loosened it, I will place its parts upon my web.

"Spider began the long and difficult task of making a web from the pinprick of light. Spider first took a strand of light and drew a line from east to west. Then Spider took another strand of light and drew a line from north to south.

"Little by little, Spider created a beautiful web of light.

"The work to make the web of light had made Spider very hungry. Spider chewed off a very tiny piece of the ball. Spider decided to take the small piece and put it on the web of light. The web of light began to grow a little brighter, and Spider began to feel refreshed.

"Spider continued to chew off bite after tiny bite.

Now the pinprick had grown large enough for Spider to look inside the ball.

"After a while, the pinprick became large enough for Spider to return inside. But the web had grown far beyond what Spider had originally woven. Just as Spider was getting ready to crawl inside the ball, white matter flew out and traveled to the farthest point north on the web. Blue matter traveled to the farthest point west. Something yellow went to the farthest point south. And something red went to the farthest point east.

"There was a loud rumbling. The deafening noise scared Spider, who scurried to the center of the web. Spider closed his eyes and curled up all eight legs. After a while, Spider's eyes opened. For as far as could be seen, millions of dots of light were captured in Spider's ever-expanding web.

"Spider decided to get closer to one of the bright dots of light. It was a slightly egg-shaped, blue-green ball that looked like Spider's home place.

"Then Spider took some of the light and spun a single line to it.

"Just as Spider let go and landed on the surface of the ball, millions of dots of light flowed from the great web. As they danced off the end of the strand, they transformed into plants and rocks and all kinds of animals. After a while, there were fewer and fewer dots of light.

"Much later, two tiny dots danced off the strand. They were the last. One transformed into a woman and the other transformed into a man. They were the first People on the land. First Woman and First Man looked at Spider and smiled. Then First Woman turned to First Man and said, 'Let us call this place Earth.'

"Spider liked that name and told First Woman and First Man that it was a good name. It was such a good name that Spider decided to stay and help the People.

"And so, it is said among the People, this is how the universe came to be and why Spider will be important to the People, always."

When the Storyteller finished his tale, no one said a word. I looked at Granma. She nodded and asked if I understood the story. The Storyteller and I looked at each other. He smiled like my granma. I closed my eyes. I was trying to decide what the truths were in the story. I opened my eyes, concentrating on the meaning buried in the Storyteller's words.

There was Spider. Granma had told me that Spider was not called he or she. Just Spider.

I couldn't help grinning when I figured out the first truth. Patience. Spider was patient and spent a lot of time thinking. Then there was the concept of biting off more than you could chew. Granma was always harping on that. Spider took a risk by climbing out of the ball. Risk-taking was another truth.

Maybe stories are so powerful because they can have so many meanings and contain so many truths.

The summer wind sent fire sparks up into the night sky, like fireflies dancing. I looked at Granma. She was using telepathy with me. She asked again if I understood the story, and I answered, "I think I do. At least the important things." The summer wind had indeed brought something very good: Somehow I knew that someday I, too, would be a Storyteller . . . to celebrate all of creation, seen and unseen.

Drum Kiss

SUSAN POWER

Even though I am eleven years old, which Grandma Lizzie says means I am practically a woman, I'm still looking for the entrance to another world at the back of her closet. I read these books by an Englishman named C. S. Lewis, my favorite one being *The Lion, the Witch, and the Wardrobe,* where four children find their way to a country called Narnia by walking into a large wardrobe and wading through the fur coats stored inside. Grandma Lizzie and I don't have a wardrobe, I don't think I've ever seen one in real life, we don't have fur coats, and there's just one clothes closet in our basement apartment, but I check it out every night before going to bed. This act is the moment of possible magic I live for, and my heart pounds every time I open the heavy door and step inside, hands groping forward in the dark to part our few garments hanging there before me, fingers tingling with excitement as they stretch and reach, poke past the clothes, stretch and reach again, only to graze the pebbly painted wall at the back. I haven't found the portal yet, but still I believe. I believe in magic and miracles and ghosts and witches. I believe there has to be a way out of this place. It's not that I would leave Grandma Lizzie behind forever. If I found my way into what the books call a "magical realm," I'd work to discover a potion that would cure my grandmother, and I'd bring it back to her and spoon it in her mouth. I would be a princess by this time, so she would listen to me and drink what I asked her to, without questions. She would obey me because she would hear the grand authority in my voice, the confidence, the kindness, the shining intelligence. Then Grandma Lizzie would be transformed into her younger self—the one I have spied in her photograph albums. I picture her the way she looked at a fancy nightclub costume party where she dressed as one of those Spanish dancers who does the flamenco, wearing a long, tight dress with tiny polka dots on the fabric and huge foamy ruffles at the hem. Her hair was pulled back in a bun framed by large tortoiseshell combs, and she'd pasted dramatic curls of hair to her forehead. Her hands were in motion, though she was posing for the camera, fingers clicking castanets so energetically I could always *hear* them when I peeked at the peeling photograph. So this is the Grandma I would win back from old age and pain; no more blindness from a white blanket of cataracts, no more arthritis that makes her fingers look all knobby and stiff as wood, makes her back and legs seize up and cock her forward so she stoops and shuffles. I know I will find the magic someday, as long as I don't give up hope and stop looking for it. But it's hard sometimes, and soon I will be twelve.

I read a lot, more than anyone else I know, which is probably why I have to wear glasses even though I'm still a girl. The frames are black and shaped like wings, and make my eyes look big and watery like black ponds. I've been reading about orphans lately, books like *Oliver Twist* and *Jane Eyre*. They're always English, it seems, and never Winnebago like me. Grandma Lizzie is from Wisconsin Dells and says that is where our people are from, going way back, but she's lived in Chicago for most of her life, and I've lived here forever. I was born in a stalled car that got stuck in a blizzard on Lake Shore Drive. My dad was trying his best to get Mom to a hospital—he'd borrowed the car—but a snowstorm fell on the city and covered it so quickly people were stuck in their cars and offices and homes, and even in stores and theaters. And it must have felt like another kind of magic—the scary kind where you realize that people are not in charge the way we think we are; there are spirits that can smother our cities or shake them loose, or shoot at us with lightning cannons in the sky. So I was a small blue icicle-Popsicle baby born in an old Ford—a car that brought life. And it was to be a car that snatched lives away from me too, like it all had to balance out in the end, the giving and taking. My parents were killed in a car accident everyone later blamed on a

Wisconsin fog. They'd been to a powwow in Black River Falls, leaving me with Grandma since I was just a baby sick with a flu. That fog confused them somehow, until they couldn't tell the road from the tree line, and they ended up driving into a wall of pines. I was too little to cry about it then, and now I never cry about my parents because I don't think of them as dead at all. Grandma Lizzie and I have been to powwows in Wisconsin, and riding in the backseat of cars we've been through some of those same smoky fogs, and twice I've seen deer step out of the steamy clouds to stare at us, at our muffled lights. And I've thought that that's what my parents are doing now, wandering the roads as bold, graceful deer, shredding the fog with their antlers, looking for me and looking for me because they love me.

Every day before I walk to school, I comb Grandma Lizzie's hair and make sure her clothes are tidy. She looks old, so old, even though she doesn't have many wrinkles, and she appears angry all the time, grumpy, since her body aches and pinches. She has silver-gray hair the color of the shiny new double-decker I.C. trains, and she keeps it short, in what she calls a "pixie cut." Grandma doesn't wear any of those fragrances that come out of a bottle, and she's clean as rain, but there's an old lady smell that covers her, trails her, sweet like cough syrup, thick and dank like rotting leaves. I guess I wear her scent on me, too, according to some of the kids at school, especially big-mouthed Tracy Martin who calls me "Grandma Stinky," instead of my true name: Fawn. At lunchtime she wrinkles her nose when I walk past her table in the cafeteria and says, "I smell Grandma Stinky. Eeuuww, she's gonna ruin my lunch with her stink!" She has such a little bitty nose in her pink face I marvel she can catch a whiff of anything at all, let alone me, just minding my own business, lunch bag in one hand and book in the other. Sometimes she'll leave her own food, a thermos of alphabet soup, a carton of chocolate milk, cookies, and a sandwich with the crusts all cut off the white Wonder Bread, and she'll come to my table when I sit by myself, and stand and look over my shoulder. She never touches me or my food, but she likes to tell everybody else what I've packed in my paper sack—most often a small box of dry cereal and a piece of fruit with spots and bruises, like a brown banana, cheaper since we bought it off the sales cart.

When Tracy makes fun of my lunch, I never feel bad on my own account, though to be honest I'd like to mush the banana in her face. Instead I want to cry for Grandma Lizzie, who spends hours every day beading earrings and bracelets and barrettes we will sell at powwows, even though the needlework hurts her hands and takes so much time because she can't see what she is doing. I've separated the tiny cut beads by color and placed them in different bowls in a certain order she has memorized. So she does it all by feel and imagination, making sparkling jewelry in her endless dark. She refuses to apply for Welfare or food stamps, which is why we eat worse than mice and all my clothes hang on me like I'm a broomstick girl with great ugly doorknobs for knees, and wool kneesocks that slide down my skinny legs and won't stay up. I want to yell at Tracy: "My grandma does the best she can, so you just shut up! Shut up before I hurt you!" But I never say these things. I just open my book to wherever I left off, and read and read, ferociously, desperately.

It's mainly the white kids who are mean to me and say stupid things; the other Indian kids in my grade will stand up for me if it looks like someone's going to push me around or beat me up, but they don't like me either since I'm always lost in a book rather than playing softball or basketball, or smoking cigarettes behind the gym. They pretty much ignore me unless I get in real trouble. I long to be friends with Gladys Green Deer, or Glad Bags, as her buddies call her. She is tall and beautiful, especially when I've seen her at powwows wearing her traditional Winnebago ribbon-work dress, and beaded moccasins that have pointy toes and a flap folded over the arches. Her earlobes are crowded with long silver earrings, and the eagle feather she pins in her hair is perfect and straight. She is so neat, so pretty, she almost doesn't look real, but more like a character set loose from one of my books. At school she just wears jeans, and her hair is loose rather than arranged in one thick braid, but she's still lovely, and graceful on the basketball court. She can blow perfect smoke rings with her Lucky Strikes, and swear harder than any of the boys. She can pin a girl to the ground in two or three seconds flat, something she's done to Tracy on several occasions, and she speaks fluent Ho Chunk just like me, the language of our tribesmen and ancestors. I want to be friends with Gladys, but I can tell I bore her. I never know what to say when she calls out a greeting. I just duck my head in a nod and smile.

Nearly every weekend there's a powwow at the American Indian Center, a huge old building on Wilson Avenue that used to be a Masonic lodge, so it's full of secret passageways and hidden rooms. Most times we dance in the gym that is also a theater with a stage set against the eastern wall. Opposite the stage, overlooking the enormous, high-ceilinged room, is a balcony the director always keeps locked. I've never been up there myself, even though I've been coming to the Center my whole life. There's an odd thing about the balcony that kids before me discovered: If you knock on the bolted door that leads to the second-floor perch, then press your ear against the rough wood and wait a few seconds, you'll hear a stirring and thumping, like a person roused to his feet, approaching the stairs that lead to the door and your straining ear. The noises aren't loud or obvious, and it can be hard to catch them at all over the music and pounding drum, but there is always a response, never just a silence in answer to a knock. The night watchman has seen strange flashing lights and disappearing figures, so we are all convinced the building is haunted.

The night of the Center Halloween party Grandma Lizzie has dressed like a cat in a fuzzy black sweater and a headband I rigged up with black pipe cleaners to make it look like she has pointy cat ears rising from her head. I drew whiskers and a black nose on her face with a kohl makeup pencil I borrowed from one of her old lady friends who has no eyebrows and paints them on each day.

"How do I look?" Grandma Lizzie asks me before we head out to catch our bus to the Indian Center. Grandma wriggles her nose like a rabbit.

"Well, you *look* like a cat, but you're not acting like one," I scold her.

"Okay, how's this?" Grandma pretends to lick her hand and wash behind the stand-up wire ears. Then she rubs her chin against the door frame.

"Better, much better."

"Okay, Your Highness, let's get this show on the road."

Grandma can't see my outfit, but I've told her how I made myself a crown out of cardboard and glitter. She let me borrow one of her gauzy party dresses from another time, one that falls to my ankles and almost hides my scuffed loafers. So here I am, transformed into a princess with eyeglasses and long black hair. I am the Princess Fawn.

At the party I eat so much candy—Indian corn and Milk Duds and Three Musketeers bars—I feel queasy and can't dance anymore. I see Gladys and a few of her friends clustered around the door to the balcony, ears against its surface. Clearly they've been trying to summon the ghost. I edge toward them, acting casual, but am nearly trampled in the stampede once they hear the faint noises on the other side. Lanky Winnebago and Chippewa girls gallop away from the balcony door like skittish colts bolting in a storm. They crash into me and drag me along with them, like a fish snagged in their net. We run out of the Indian Center, escaping through the doors on the western side of the building, where there are steps with handrails we like to slide down. Gladys is in charge, as usual, pacing, musing aloud about who the ghost could be.

"Do you think it's one of those old Masons who broke some kind of trust so they walled him up in there and starved him to death? Or is it Vivian's son who died that time from sniffing glue?"

There is a chatter of voices as girls pipe up with their suggestions. I hear a soft low voice that is quieter than the others but more confident, measured, and it takes me by surprise to realize this is my own voice wedging itself into their circle.

"This isn't just a ghost story," I'm telling the girls, "it's also a romantic one. A story of hillbilly love."

"*Hill*billy *love*," Gladys snorts with contempt. "How do you figure *that* happened?" She isn't just poking fun at my opening line, she's curious, too, I can tell. So I find the courage to continue.

I invent a story I have no idea was cooking inside me. This is what I tell them: "A few years back there was a girl named Ronnie, who was sixteen years old and had just moved here with her family from the Appalachian Mountains southeast of here. She had some cousins in Uptown and they showed her the ropes when she arrived, and took her to the Center for the pinball machines in the basement, and the bingo on Sundays, and the free food at powwows. She met one of those Fun Maker boys from the Dells, you know how tall and handsome they are? Well, she met one of them, Kunu, and fell madly in love with him. The kind of crazy love where you can't eat and you can't sleep and you can hardly even breathe. Ronnie had wavy gold hair that fell to her ankles, long as Rita Coolidge's hair, and big green eyes, and the longest eye-lashes, and when she looked up at Kunu a certain way he fell in love too. You'd think that would be that, except both their parents disapproved of their relationship, hers and his. She decided to turn Indian as much as she could because our ways aren't so different from theirs, but there were just a lot of things she didn't know, such as the drum being off-limits to women, being an energy she shouldn't mess with. She loved to hear Kunu sit in at the drum with his uncles and brothers and cousins, and sing so high and so hard. She would stand behind him and lean forward to hear his voice untangled from the rest. And one time, at a Center powwow, after everybody was in line getting their dinner, she knelt down to touch the drum and, more than that, she kissed the spot on the hide that was faded, the decorative paint rubbed off from the pounding of Kunu's drumstick. Nobody saw her do it, nobody was paying any attention to her, but later she told Kunu she'd kissed his drum to show her devotion, and it was only then she learned what a dangerous thing she had done. Kunu wouldn't kiss her good night after the dance, he just left with his family, and she sat outside the Center on these steps, her head on her arms, crying and crying because she hadn't meant to break a taboo and anger the love of her life. She had nearly cried herself out when she felt warm breath on her neck that chilled her and excited her at the same time. He must have come back, she was thinking, and lifted her head to see if it was really Kunu there beside her. But she couldn't see *any*thing, *any*one, just felt the warm wet breath, and then a sucking mouth that slipped from the back of her neck to the side, where her pulsing artery fluttered beneath her skin. The entire neighborhood heard a horrible scream and then dead silence, and it was so awful, dozens of people called the police. They found her in the moonlight, laid out on these steps with her hair running every which way like melted gold. Her green eyes were bulging, staring at the sky, and several policemen slipped on the steps because they were so slick with blood from the wound at her throat where a vengeful spirit had torn it out, her life along with it. My grandma taught me you have to be careful not to anger the spirits or they will punish you in terrible ways. Ronnie's ghost could probably move on if she wanted, but she stays here, looking for Kunu, waiting for him to join her. That's why he doesn't come around the Center so much anymore. He's probably afraid she'll come after him just like the spirit came after her, and eat him, too, like a wolf. She lives up on that balcony and hangs over the edge, tears falling on us, and whenever we knock on her door she starts down, full of hope and dread at the same time—hopeful it will be her love, afraid it will just be us kids."

I stopped talking and found myself the center of attention, an awed silence wrapped around me like one of Grandma Lizzie's old blankets.

"Ronnie, huh?" Gladys finally said. "Not too bad, Fawn. I liked your story."

I have friends now, Gladys Green Deer and her crowd, and Tracy Martin still calls me names, but it doesn't bother me anymore. Even the newest taunt, "Roach Girl," can't bring me down. It's true that Grandma Lizzie and I have a cockroach problem—those little suckers are fearless and determined, and no matter how many Roach Motels I set up to trap them, there's always another crew to replace the last. What they feed on I don't know, since we never have much in the way of groceries, and what we *do* have we keep in the refrigerator, but they share our space undiscouraged by the slim pickings we have to offer. I snap out my clothes before dressing to make sure I'm insect-free when I leave our place, but the other day I forgot, and there I was, walking past Tracy, when one little specimen scuttled from the breast pocket of my dress and made her scream.

"*Ugh!* You disgusting thing!" she shouted at me. "Roach Girl. Roach Girl. Look out for the incredible Roach Girl!"

My Indian friends just shrugged their shoulders because they fight the same battle I do with the bugs and rodents, so it wasn't like news. When I am a princess, I will, of course, have exterminators, so this will no longer be a problem.

I go to sleepover parties at Gladys's place, where we watch Creature Feature horror movies and eat this cool new cereal called Count Chocula. I tell the girls stories before we fall asleep, and no one thinks I'm boring anymore. But some of the stories I keep for myself—like the actual version regarding the ghost in the balcony. I have my own secret idea that Ronnie is just a fiction my imagination pumped into my head. She never really existed beyond my words. I don't think there is only one ghost living behind the balcony door, but two. And they are beautiful spirits surrounded by fog, come to the end of a journey traveled gracefully by night on the roads and highways that lead from Black River Falls to Chicago. And the noises we hear are their hooves and their antlers, because this time they have come back as deer, their eyes as black and watery as my own appear behind the glasses I wear. I believe my parents have found me in Chicago, in this Uptown neighborhood where I live with Grandma. They looked for me and looked for me, because they love me. I believe in them and magic and miracles, and it is all a little easier to have faith in now that I am twelve.

ABOUT THE AUTHORS

Sherman Alexie, a Spokane-Coeur d'Alene poet, novelist, and filmmaker, grew up in Wellpinit, Washington, on the Spokane Indian Reservation. Among his many books are *The Business of Fancydancing* (which is also the title of a film that he directed), *Reservation Blues, Indian Killer, Ten Little Indians*, and *The Lone Ranger and Tonto Fistfight in Heaven*. He lives in Seattle, Washington.

Joseph Bruchac is a prolific author and poet whose work draws on his Native American heritage and especially on stories that he heard from his Abenaki grandfather. Although his Indian heritage is only part of an ethnic background that includes Slovak and English, his Native roots are deepest and he has cultivated them the most. He is the founder of the Greenfield Review Press. Among his published works are *Entering Onondaga, Thirteen Moons on Turtle's Back, Skeleton Man, The Dark Pond*, and *Keepers of the Earth*. He lives in the Adirondack foothills of upstate New York.

Louise Erdrich grew up in North Dakota and is a member of the Turtle Mountain Band of Ojibwe. She is the author of twelve novels for adults, three books of poetry, several children's books, and a memoir of early motherhood. Her fiction appears regularly in *The New Yorker*. She lives in Minnesota and owns a small independent bookstore, Birchbark Books.

Lee Francis (Laguna Pueblo) was national director of Wordcraft Circle of Native Writers and Storytellers. The vision of this organization, with members throughout Indian Country (Native and non-Native) is "to ensure that the voices of Native writers and storytellers—past, present, and future—are heard throughout the world." Francis, who held a Ph.D., was also tenured associate professor of Native American Studies at the University of New Mexico until his death in 2003. Among his works were *Native Time: A Historical Time Line of Native America* and a book of poetry, *On the Good Red Interstate: Truck Stop Tellings and Other Poems*.

Joy Harjo was born in Tulsa, Oklahoma, and is an enrolled member of the Muscogee Nation. An award-winning writer and member of the National Council on the Arts, her many books of poetry include *The Last Song, What Moon Drove Me to This?, The Woman Who Fell from the Sky, A Map to the Next World*, and the children's book *The Good Luck Cat*. In addition, she performs nationally and internationally with her band, Joy Harjo and Poetic

Justice, for which she plays saxophone. Currently she divides her time between Hawaii and California.

Linda Hogan, a Chickasaw poet, novelist, and essayist, is a professor at the University of Colorado. She is the recipient of an American Book Award, an NEA grant, a Lannan Award, and a Guggenheim Fellowship. She is the author of, among other books, *The Woman Who Watches Over the World*, *Dwellings: A Spiritual History of the Living World*, *Mean Spirit*, and the novel *Power*.

Susan Power (Standing Rock Sioux) is the author of *Roofwalker* as well as *The Grass Dancer*, winner of the 1995 PEN/Hemingway Award. She is a graduate of Harvard College, Harvard Law School, and the Iowa Writers' Workshop, and the recipient of a James Michener Fellowship, Radcliffe Bunting Institute Fellowship, and Princeton Hodder Fellowship. Her fiction has been published in *The Atlantic Monthly*, *The Paris Review*, and *Story* magazine, among others, and has been selected for inclusion in *The Best American Short Stories*. Power resides in St. Paul, Minnesota.

Greg Sarris, part American Indian, Filipino, and Jewish, was adopted at birth and raised in both Indian and white families. He is the author of *Mabel McKay: Weaving the Dream* and the novel *Grand Avenue*, and the editor of *Rattles and Clappers*. Formerly the elected chief of the Miwok tribe, Greg Sarris is currently a professor of English at UCLA and lives in Los Angeles.

Cynthia Leitich Smith was raised in northeastern Kansas and is a mixed blood, enrolled member of the Muscogee Nation. Among her publications are the young adult novel *Rain Is Not My Indian Name*; a chapter book, *Indian Shoes*; and a picture book, *Jingle Dancer*. Before turning to writing full time, she worked as a reporter for several newspapers and then as an attorney. Today she lives in Austin, Texas, with her husband and two gray tabby cats. She runs a very popular children's book review website, www.cynthialeitichsmith.com.

Richard Van Camp is a member of the Dogrib (Tlicho) Nation. He was born and raised in Fort Smith in the Northwest Territories of Canada. He is the author of a novel, *The Lesser Blessed,* a collection of short stories, *Angel Wing Splash Pattern,* and two children's books illustrated by Cree artist George Littlechild: *A Man Called Raven* and *What's the Most Beautiful Thing You Know About Horses?* He teaches creative writing for aboriginal students at the University of British Columbia in Vancouver, British Columbia. You can visit him at www.richardvancamp.org.